PUFFIN BOOKS

THE LOST PRINCE

V. M. Jones lives in Christchurch, New Zealand, with her husband and two sons. Her previous novels are *Buddy*, which won the Junior Fiction and Best First Book Awards in the 2003 New Zealand Post Children's Book Awards, and *Juggling with Mandarins*, winner of the 2004 Junior Fiction Award. *The Serpents of Arakesh*, the first book in The Karazan Quartet, was shortlisted for both the 2004 New Zealand Post Junior Fiction Award and the 2004 LIANZA Esther Glen Medal. *The Lost Prince* is the third book in The Karazan Quartet.

karazan.co.uk

Books by V. M. Jones

THE SERPENTS OF ARAKESH
DUNGEONS OF DARKNESS
THE LOST PRINCE
QUEST FOR THE SUN

THE LOST PRINCE

KARAZAN
The Third

V. M. JONES

PUFFIN

PUFFIN BOOKS

Published by the Penguin Group
Penguin Books Ltd, 80 Strand, London WC2R 0RL, England
Penguin Group (USA) Inc., 375 Hudson Street, New York, New York 10014, USA
Penguin Group (Canada), 90 Eglinton Avenue East, Suite 700, Toronto, Ontario, Canada M4P 2Y3
(a division of Pearson Penguin Canada Inc.)
Penguin Ireland, 25 St Stephen's Green, Dublin 2, Ireland (a division of Penguin Books Ltd)
Penguin Group (Australia), 250 Camberwell Road, Camberwell, Victoria 3124, Australia
(a division of Pearson Australia Group Pty Ltd)
Penguin Books India Pvt Ltd, 11 Community Centre, Panchsheel Park, New Delhi – 110 017, India
Penguin Group (NZ), cnr Airborne and Rosedale Roads, Albany, Auckland 1310, New Zealand
(a division of Pearson New Zealand Ltd)
Penguin Books (South Africa) (Pty) Ltd, 24 Sturdee Avenue, Rosebank, Johannesburg 2196, South Africa

Penguin Books Ltd, Registered Offices: 80 Strand, London WC2R 0RL, England

www.penguin.com

First published in New Zealand by HarperCollins Publishers (New Zealand) Ltd 2004
First published in Great Britain in Puffin Books 2006
1

Text copyright © V. M. Jones, 2004
Illustrations copyright © Christopher Downes, 2004

The moral right of the author and illustrator has been asserted

Set in 11.5/15.5 pt Monotype Plantin
Typeset by Rowland Phototypesetting Ltd, Bury St Edmunds, Suffolk
Made and printed in England by Clays Ltd, St Ives plc

British Library Cataloguing in Publication Data
A CIP catalogue record for this book is available from the British Library

ISBN-13: 978-0-141-31944-5
ISBN-10: 0-141-31944-5

To D – always and forever

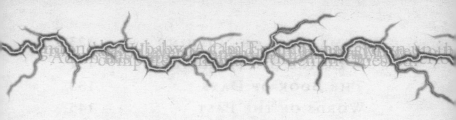

CONTENTS

PROLOGUE

They drifted into the throne room like shadows. With them came a sudden darkness, and a chill as if a cloud had passed over the face of the sun.

Instantly, there was silence.

In their annex the queens shrank away, covering their faces. At a gesture from the hunched, misshapen figure beside the throne, pages sprang forward and drew the heavy drapes to screen them.

The sorcerer hobbled forward, peering from his nest of tangled hair. With each step the heavy folds of his purple gown flapped grotesquely, like the wings of a crippled bird. 'Clear the throne room,' he croaked.

In moments, only the hooded figures of the Faceless and the sorcerer remained. They . . . and the king. He lay back on the low couch that was his throne, as still as a gilded statue. His expression seemed unchanged, but deep in his eyes something flickered for a moment, bright and hungry as a flame. Only Evor the sorcerer knew it for what it was: white-hot anger, hope, and perhaps most of all . . . fear.

Evor spoke for the king. 'Well? Where are they?'

The leading figure came to a standstill some distance from the throne, the others shuffling up behind it like ragged vultures closing on a kill. There was a pause; then the loose, rattling choke of what had once been a voice, coughing its way through rotting vocal chords. 'Gone.'

'*Gone?* What do you mean, gone? Gone where? Where could they go?'

'Portal.' The word was spat into the silence like a thick gob of phlegm.

'You lost them.' The accusation hissed through the air like a whip. 'All of them.'

'Not all.' The leader of the Faceless withdrew something from deep within its cloak and dropped it at the sorcerer's feet.

Evor stared down at it. It was the size of a newborn baby, limp and boneless as a corpse. The skinny body was covered in fine, silky fur, except for its bright blue rump and the smooth, hairless face, shrunken and pathetic, clenched in a frozen rictus of almost human horror.

Evor turned the body over with his foot, considering. 'This was travelling with them?'

There was an almost imperceptible movement within the dark hood.

'Is it dead?'

'No, my lord.' Evor bent and lifted the limp form by its neck, the head lolling uselessly. 'It has breathed the chill of the grave, but it lives.'

The king's cold gaze flicked from the leader of the Faceless to the shadowy figures behind, resting on them one by one. 'You have failed me,' he said softly. 'It will not happen again, or you will be returned to the depths from which you came. Be gone.'

'Now,' murmured Evor, 'now, my lord, let us see what the Faceless have delivered us.' He crouched beside the king, cradling the limp form in the crook of one arm like a baby. The low table before the throne carried an array of delicate phials, as well as another object, small, dark and compact, looking strangely out of place among the gleaming crystal.

Evor's hand hovered above the phials for a moment before settling on one filled with a phosphorescent liquid like mother-of-pearl. He withdrew the crystal stopper from its neck, put his finger over the opening, and tilted the bottle. A single drop of potion gleamed like a pearl on the end of his gnarled and twisted finger. He inserted one long fingernail between the creature's lips and levered the mouth open, then touched the tip of his finger to its tongue.

Both sorcerer and king watched intently. For a long moment, nothing happened. Then the tight-clenched eyelids relaxed, and both bright button eyes flickered open. Blinked, focused on the face of the sorcerer centimetres from its own – and squeezed instantly shut again.

Evor's breath wheezed out in what might almost have been a laugh. 'You may seek to hide yourself in darkness, but the darkness will not hide you. There is no refuge for you now.'

The king reached forward and touched the line where the smooth skin met the ruff of fur surrounding the small face. When he spoke, his voice was as caressing as the finger had been. 'What were you once, little chatterbot? And here, among friends . . . what might you become?'

'We shall see.' Evor reached for another phial, upended it, and shook it over the still form of the little monkey. As the fine droplets touched its face it flinched slightly; then its body rippled in a long, convulsive shudder. Evor set it gently down on the carpet in front of the throne.

For a moment, the chatterbot's entire body seemed to vibrate. Then its limbs began to twitch and jerk. The face contorted, the slit mouth opening in an inaudible scream. And then, in a series of anguished, heaving convulsions, the tiny body began to stretch and grow. The furry coat smoothed, the silky fibres melting away; the arms and legs straightened and extended; the face flattened and stretched. The long, prehensile tail telescoped away to nothing. There was a single shrill, jibbering shriek that faded to a series of moaning sobs . . . and then the ragged, pyjama-clad form of a boy was lying sprawled on the red carpet, pain and confusion giving way to fear in his wide brown eyes.

With a sudden scramble he twisted onto all fours, crouching like an animal at bay, teeth bared. Evor took a lurching step forward, and the boy threw up one hand in an instinctive gesture of self-defence . . . and saw his own pyjama-clad arm in front of his face. His eyes widened, and his mouth fell open in an expression of almost comical shock. He looked at his hand, turned it, opened and closed the smooth, pink fingers. Stumbled to his feet, staring down at his straight boy's body in disbelief. Looked from Evor to the king, and back again. His mouth opened. 'Y-you . . . I . . .'

'What is done can equally be undone,' hissed Evor, 'and what is undone need not be undone for all eternity. We know now *what* you are. *Who* you are, we will soon discover.'

'N-no.' The boy's voice shook slightly. 'I'm not going to tell you anyfing.'

'Be still, Evor. Come now, little one.' The king's voice was soft as velvet. 'You need not be afraid. I am King Karazeel, and this is my trusted servant Evor. Tell us your name. There can be no harm in that. See, Evor has returned you to your natural form. Is that not evidence enough of our good will?'

The boy blinked and shook his head. 'I dunno . . . maybe. I . . . I guess so. My name . . . my name's Bl- . . . I mean, Weevil. William Weaver, I mean . . . Your Worship.'

King Karazeel's lips twitched. 'There now. Was that so hard? Bravely said. You see – all is well. Welcome to Shakesh, William Weaver. And now . . .'

But the boy's eyes had fallen on the object that lay

5

on the table beside the crystal phials. Instantly they widened, and his face broke into a grin. 'Hey!' he blurted, the words spilling from his mouth the second the thought was fully formed in his mind. 'A computer! I –' Then he realised what he'd said. His hand flew to his mouth, as if to snatch the words back . . . but it was too late. They hung in the air of the throne room like iridescent bubbles, way beyond reach.

'So.' The king's voice was very soft. 'It is a *computer*. I see. Yes, I think I begin to see. And tell me, my little friend: you seem like such a clever boy. What more can you tell us about this *computer*? Its purpose, perhaps? Its . . . powers? But no – you are too young for such wisdom.'

A flush spread over the boy's pale face. 'Too young?' he said indignantly. 'That's what you fink! I know *heaps* about computers – more than most grown-ups. They're my fing. I could tell you more about computers than practically anyone on earth – if I wanted to,' he amended hurriedly. 'But I don't – and you can't make me.'

King Karazeel and Evor looked at each other . . . and smiled.

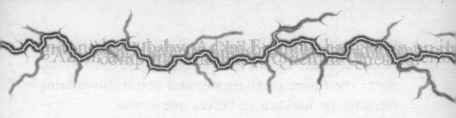

TOO GOOD TO LAST

The bucket chairs had been arranged in a long line stretching right down the corridor from Matron's office door almost as far as the rec room.

I still thought of it as Matron's office . . . and looking at the closed door still gave me that familiar helpless, queasy feeling, even though I knew she'd never be back.

Every ten minutes or so the door would open a crack and one of the kids would sidle out. Then whoever was at the front of the line would get up and go into the office and close the door behind them, and we'd all shift up one seat closer, onto a grey plastic seat warm from the previous person's bum.

It was hard to read the expressions of the kids coming out of Matron's office. They seemed guarded – wary, almost. They looked down at the floor and said nothing.

Behind the office door was Mr Smigielski. 'His name is pronounced ShmeegYELLskee,' Cookie had told us at breakfast, dishing up fried eggs and bacon.

'He's the Chairman of the Board of Trustees, and he'll be coming after school today to talk to you individually about the future of Highgate, and about the exciting plans he has for each and every one of you.'

Her words had seemed real upbeat and positive, and some of the littler kids gave each other sparkly looks and jiggled up and down on their chairs. Not me. I looked at the way Cook's mouth was tucked in at the corners, and how she was staring down at the pile of bacon instead of up at us while she talked . . . and I couldn't help noticing the way her big, pillowy front heaved in a ginormous sigh under the bib of her faded old apron.

And it made me wonder.

The door opened and Geoffrey came out, his chubby angel face blank and expressionless. He darted a glance at me, then down at the floor again, and tried to sidle past the row of chairs into the garden.

But I grabbed hold of the leg of his pants as he went past. 'Pssst, Geoffrey,' I hissed, 'what did he say? What's going on?'

Geoffrey gave me a furtive, trapped look. His rosebud mouth quivered. 'We're not allowed to say,' he whispered righteously. 'And if you don't let go of me right now, Adam Equinox, I'll *scream*.'

Hurriedly, I let go. Shifted one seat up, feeling the hot dampness where Callum's legs had been. Waited.

Highgate had been a different place since Matron left.

She'd been arrested for fraud – it turned out she'd been creaming money off the allowance meant for feeding and clothing us kids. Doing it for years, salting it all away in a secret bank account and buying stuff for herself – including a brand-new car – while we wore op-shop rags and ate food on waste from the supermarket because it was past its use-by date.

We all hoped that once Matron was safely in prison we'd inherit her DVD player and flat-screen TV, but Cookie said it had been taken away by the police as evidence. So the television was still the same junk-shop special that could only get one channel – if you were lucky.

Nothing much else had changed – on the surface, that is. There were still the same creaky old beds crammed into overcrowded dorms, the same smell of floor polish and disinfectant, the same ramshackle garden full of weeds, the same bare patches on the lawn, the same sagging clothesline billowing with threadbare sheets and ragged hand-me-downs.

But now the allowance that had been given to Matron was given to Cook – and Cookie was spending it all on us. Before, the fridges had been stacked with dripping bags of greyish meat, slimy chickens and wilted bunches of spinach. Now they were cram-jammed with packs of smoked bacon, fresh farm eggs, crispy lettuces and whole heads of celery so fresh you could snap the stalks. The vegetable rack had once held bruised apples, blackened bananas and oranges patchy with blue mould. Now it was piled with potatoes, onions and other fresh veggies, and there was a basket on the servery full of fresh fruit for us to help ourselves whenever we wanted.

Cook had started having her radio on in the kitchen while she worked, and we'd come back from school to the sound of golden oldies, Cookie singing along as she laid out our afternoon tea and started the preparations for dinner.

Before, you could tell what day of the week it was by what was on the menu. Now, it depended on what was on special at the supermarket, and what Cookie felt in the mood to make. I'd got in the habit of poking my head round the corner when I dropped off my lunch box, grabbing an apple or a pear, and asking, 'So – what's for dinner, Cookie?' You never knew what the answer would be. It could be 'roast beef and Yorkshire pudding', or 'lasagne', or 'chicken à la king' . . . or sometimes 'wait and see, you little monkey – and don't you come bothering me when I'm busy!'

Best of all was that the sense of being watched had completely disappeared. There was no sick, nervous feeling of dread that you'd be caught doing something you never even dreamed was wrong. Half the rules went out the window. We were allowed to read for fifteen minutes in bed before lights-out. We had picnics in the garden when the weather was nice. We were even encouraged to invite friends to play in the afternoon.

And we could use the computer whenever we liked, as long as no one else was rostered on.

Yeah, Highgate sure was a different place.

The door opened and Callum shuffled out. As he passed me he gave a long, liquid sniff.

I stood up and walked the two steps across to the door. My knees had the same peculiar feeling they used to have in Matron's day – as if they were slowly dissolving. Habit, I guess. I put my hand on the door-knob, same as I'd done a million times before. Turned it . . . and as the doorknob turned, so did my stomach, in a slow, sickening roll.

I gave myself a mental shake, took a deep breath, and went in.

MR SMIGIELSKI

The room was completely bare except for Matron's big desk. It had been positioned in the middle of the floor, with a plain brown Manila folder in the dead centre of its shiny wooden surface. There was a chair on my side, empty. And there was Mr Smigielski, sitting behind the desk.

He looked as if someone had put him between two sheets of tissue paper and shut him inside a book for a couple of weeks, sideways-on. His head was long and narrow, with a sharp chin and a pointy nose like a beak. His eyes were very close together and his skin an unhealthy-looking greyish colour, with a blue shadow like bruising over his cheeks and chin where he'd shaved. His hair was black – flat black like paint, so dark I almost wondered if he could have dyed it. It was combed carefully across his scalp in stripes you could have counted.

He was wearing a plain black suit and a narrow black tie. His Adam's apple jutted out above the tight knot of the tie as if he'd tried to swallow a peach stone and it had stuck halfway down.

He stared at me expressionlessly for what seemed like a long time. Then his mouth stretched into what I guessed was meant to be a smile. 'Come in and sit down.'

I shambled forward, pulled out the chair with a grating sound, and lowered myself reluctantly onto it. I was suddenly very aware of my shaggy hair, long overdue for a cut, and the rash of pimples that had recently sprouted under my greasy fringe. My hands and feet felt huge and awkward, gangling and out of proportion to the rest of me. I noticed my nails were dirty. Hastily, I tucked my hands out of sight between my knees.

Mr Smigielski had a peculiar stillness about him that reminded me of a snake. It gave me a crazy urge to fidget. But I made myself sit still and stare right back at him, into his small, opaque black eyes.

Finally, he spoke again. 'And you are?' His voice was flat-sounding too, as if it had been squashed in the book along with the rest of him.

'Adam,' I mumbled. 'Adam Equinox.' The *Adam* came out deep and gruff, but the *Equinox* notched itself up an octave into a stupid-sounding squeak. I felt myself blush, and scowled furiously down at the floor.

'Hmmm . . . Adam Equinox. An unusual name.' He flicked the folder open. Upside down, from across the desk, I couldn't see what was in it; but it didn't look to be much.

'Yeah, I guess,' I muttered.

'As you know, I am Mr Smigielski, Chairman of the Board of Trustees of Highgate. I would find it of assistance if you could give me a brief outline of your history and the circumstances of your placement here.'

'But . . . isn't it all there? In my file?'

He smiled thinly. 'Unfortunately many of the records appear to have gone astray. Personal records pertaining to residents of Highgate, as well as records of a – ah – financial nature. This applies particularly to children whose residency is longer-standing, as I believe is true of you.'

'Huh?'

'How long have you lived at Highgate, Adam?'

'My whole life.'

He made a note in black pen on a clean sheet of paper.

'And who are – or were – your parents?'

I flushed again. Even though I'd never known them, I hated the thought of talking about them to this cold-eyed stranger. 'I dunno,' I mumbled.

He capped his pen and set it down on the desk with a tiny *click*. 'Come now, Adam. Let us work together here. Cooperation will be in your own best interests, as I shall shortly make clear. Now: who were your parents, and why were you brought to live at Highgate?'

I glowered at him. 'I told you: *I don't know!*' My voice sounded rough and angry in the stillness of the room. 'I was left on the doorstep. I was less than a day

14

old. No one ever saw her . . . my mum.' My voice cracked again on the last word. 'I don't know who she was – or my dad. No one does. OK?' Glaring across the desk at him, I thought bleakly that it didn't matter much about my records going missing. Those few stark facts were all the history I had.

He nodded sadly. 'A classic scenario, alas. Yet another example of how low moral standards coupled with a complete absence of responsibility encumber charitable institutions such as this.'

It took me a second to work out what he was saying. Then I was on my feet, fists clenched, my chair crashing over onto the floor behind me. 'Listen to me, mister,' I snarled, and for once my voice stayed low and growly: 'whether I knew her or not, whether she dumped me or not, it's my mother you're talking about!'

He didn't so much as flinch. Just shook his head and sighed, as if my reaction confirmed something he'd already suspected. His pen scratched tidily across the paper again. Then he glanced up. 'So: is there nothing more?'

I shook my head. I wasn't about to tell him about the things that were with me when I was found – the shawl I'd been wrapped in, my penny whistle, and the heavy, odd-shaped ring I wore on an old bootlace round my neck. Not now, after what he'd said. No way.

'Sit down.' I picked up the chair and sat. 'No doubt you are wondering what in fact this folder *does* contain.' I hadn't been, but I had a feeling he was going to tell me anyhow. I was right. 'Your latest school report, for one thing. It describes a sullen, angry youth with a chip on his shoulder and an attitude problem.' I shrugged. I'd heard it all before.

'In addition, I have here the results of the recent aptitude test undertaken by the careers councillor at your school.'

My heart sank. I'd tried my hardest to forget about it – but I knew from long experience that things like that come back and bite you in the bum when you least expect it.

'Try to think of it in positive terms, Adam,' the guidance geezer had told me after I'd battled my way miserably through the truckload of tests. 'You have a learning *difference*, rather than a disability – a difference in the way your brain handles information other children find easy to access and process.' Well, at least now I knew why I was always bottom of the class. 'We prefer not to label children these days,' he'd gone on, scrawling MODERATELY DISABLED in red pen across the top of his report. 'I'm sure you'll find your niche in life eventually. You'll never be a rocket scientist, of course – *haw haw* – but there are other, more practically-based options. Everyone is good at something, you know – or so we must keep telling ourselves. You scored quite highly on the leadership scale, relatively speaking,' he'd finished off doubtfully.

My friend Cameron had bounced out of the interview room with his specs misted over with excitement, babbling away about subject choices and universities and whether he'd eventually opt for law or medicine. But then he noticed I was quieter than usual, and peered anxiously at me. 'How about you, Adam?' he asked. 'What did Mr Guthrie say about *your* future?' I didn't want to burst Cam's bubble by telling him the truth: that I didn't seem to have one.

And now Mr Smigielski was skimming through the report, shaking his head and tut-tutting. 'I don't see what all this has got to do with Highgate,' I muttered. I'd almost said 'with *you*,' but stopped myself in time. 'With the . . . the future, and what's going to happen now Matron's gone, and all that.'

'It is relevant,' he said frostily, tearing himself away from my report. 'Highly relevant, I am afraid.' He put his long, narrow fingers together to form a steeple, and watched me over it. 'You see, Adam, Highgate is to close down. Alternative arrangements are to be made for the children: foster homes and adoption, wherever possible. The normal criteria for prospective guardians will be substantially relaxed to increase the chances of success. We call it *Positive Placement Policy*; it has worked most effectively in the past.'

He smiled thinly.

'Some children, however,' and he tapped my file lightly with his pen, 'are harder to place than others.

'And some – alas – prove impossible.'

POSITIVE PLACEMENT POLICY

The world as I knew it came crashing down around my ears.

In my heart, I'd hoped maybe Cookie would be given Matron's job, and we'd all live happily ever after.

But life isn't a fairy tale.

I don't know how long it was before I realised Mr Smigielski was still talking away, as matter-of-fact and unemotional as if he was reading a shopping list.

My mind reeling, I tuned back in. 'We will leave no stone unturned in our quest for suitable homes for you children. Naturally, our first port of call will be relatives – even a biological parent, once traced, may prove to be in a situation enabling them to revisit the issue of parenthood. Other than that . . . well, under normal circumstances we would insist on married couples within a certain age range, carefully screened for suitability. But as I have mentioned, under the Positive Placement Policy, virtually anyone prepared to take on the responsibility of guardianship will be considered. I am constantly astonished by how many people long for a child. There are godparents, aunts, grandparents, even family friends . . . in most cases, that is. But not in yours.

'I will be frank with you, Adam. Your solitary state in the world will not count in your favour. Neither will your track record, your learning disability, your gender, your age, or, I regret to say, your appearance. Puberty is an unsavoury stage, even in one's own children. It would take a remarkable person – almost a saint, dare I say – to take a boy such as you under their wing.

'Yes, painful though it is for me to admit it, your chances of adoption – or even of a medium-term fostering arrangement – are marginal, to put it kindly.'

I stared at him. I felt as if I was falling into a bottom-less void. Where there had once been solid ground – rough ground, but solid – now there was nothing. Highgate – closing? Why? What about Cookie? But most of all . . .

'What then?' I croaked. 'What if you're right, and no one takes me in? Where will I go? What will happen to me?'

He smiled, his eyes like black pebbles. 'There is no cause for alarm. The Board will continue to honour its obligations to its dependants, should any remain. There is another orphanage which falls under the auspices of the Trust. It is situated some distance from here, on the coast.' For a second, I felt a flicker of hope. The seaside! 'However, we should regard it as a last resort,' he continued. 'The rocky peninsula on which it is sited is not without a certain dramatic appeal, but the building itself is older, and somewhat austere. Yes, unfortunately there can be no doubt that Rippingale Hall lacks many of the modern comforts and additional facilities you enjoy at Highgate.' What was he talking about? What modern comforts? What additional facilities? The television? The tool shed? But if it was worse than Highgate . . .

'Why does it have to close?' Even to me, my voice sounded squeaky and pathetic. 'Highgate, I mean?' Half an hour ago, I'd have thought Highgate closing would be the best news ever. Not now – now that it was actually happening.

For a moment, something flickered deep in his eyes. 'You would not be aware of the fact, but this building is situated on an extremely valuable piece of real estate, young man. In the current market, demolition, subdivision and redevelopment is the logical way forward.' He was leaning across the table now, and as he spoke little flecks of spit landed on the polished surface between us. 'Yes,' he continued, 'in a year's time an exclusive residential subdivision named Highgate Hills will stand where this building and its grounds do now . . . and I . . .'

'You?'

'I shall have discharged my duties to the Trust, and will stand down to pursue . . . other interests.'

'But Cookie . . .'

'The cook has been given one month's notice,' he said coldly, 'as laid down in her contract.

'Send the next child in.'

I am at Quested Court, playing hide and seek with Hannah – and Tiger Lily and Bluebell too, of course.

I'm hunting for Hannah in her bedroom – and I know she's somewhere there. I look in the cupboards, one by one. Under the four-poster bed. Behind the chair. Then I hear a stifled giggle. It's coming from the big wooden toy box. I tiptoe up to it, hesitate, grinning to myself. 'Don't be so dumb, Adam,' I say out loud, so she can hear. 'She couldn't possibly fit in there – not a big girl like Hannah!' I allow her a long moment of delicious suspense . . . then lift the lid. Sure enough, there she is: scrunched up with her knees around her ears and a cat on either side purring fit to bust. Then she's out of there, hopping up and down and squeaking, 'Your turn, Adam! Your turn to hide!'

She covers her eyes and starts to count.

I race off and up the wide staircase. As I climb it starts to narrow and twist. The broad carpeted treads shrink down to dark stone wedges, crumbling at the edges. I run on up the spiral stairway, stumble, fall. Scrabble the last few metres on hands and knees, my breath rasping in my throat; clamber to my feet and stumble down the dark corridor, scanning the dripping walls desperately for somewhere to hide.

At last I see a door recessed into the stone. There's no doorknob, only a tiny keyhole almost blocked with rust. Footsteps echo down the corridor after me. I know the

21

door will be locked, but I push it anyway. It swings open.
Behind it is a tiny room, the size of a broom cupboard,
pitch dark. I squeeze inside, heart hammering, and push
the door closed again behind me.

I wait in the darkness.

Footsteps, growing closer. Heavy, slow footsteps. Foot-
steps that could never belong to Hannah. They stop outside
the door. I wait, the blood pounding in my ears.

A voice reaches me, muffled by the stone. A deep voice,
strangely familiar, but somehow smudged, the words
dragged out ghoulishly like a tape recording on slow. The
words are my own, but I feel the hair on my neck stand up
at the sound of them.

'He couldn't possibly fit in here – not a big boy like
Adam.'

The door creaks slowly open.

Shaw is staring down at me, smiling.

'Why, 'ello there, Adam,' he says. 'Wot in tarnation
are you doin' 'ere at Quested Court?'

I shuffle out of the cubbyhole, blushing, feeling like a
prize idiot. 'D-didn't you know, Shaw?' I hear myself
stammer. 'Q . . . he adopted me. Remember?'

Shaw looks down at me, and slowly, pityingly, shakes
his head. The face is Shaw's, but the eyes are flat and un-
readable . . . and suddenly, horrifyingly, the voice is Q's.

'No, dear boy, I'm afraid you're wrong. I adopted
Geoffrey.'

My eyes jerked open. The shock of Q's words rang in
my head. My heart was thudding sickeningly in my

chest, and a tinny taste like shroud was on my tongue.

It was a dream, I told myself roughly. *Only a dumb dream.* But behind that voice was another one, harsher still.

And you were dumb to dream it.

I lay on my back staring at the patterns made by the moonlight shining through the leaves of the tree outside. The thick stripes of the bars – to keep burglars out, us in – looked black and solid beside the watery, shifting shadows. But I ignored the bars and focused on the leaves.

Watching them, I gradually felt my heartbeat slow and my breath come deep and even. My skin felt cool and smooth under the thin, scratchy blanket.

In my mind, I answered the second voice.

It's never dumb to dream. Sometimes you have to dream – just to keep going.

Lying there, I acknowledged the truth at last. Examined it, turning it carefully this way and that.

Yes. Deep down inside me was a longing – a yearning so strong it was almost an ache – for something I knew I could never have. It was a longing to be part of the life I'd had a taste of at Quested Court, with Hannah and Q. If I could have anything in the world, it would be that.

Not the luxury; the love.

But it was a world I could never belong to, except for a week here and there if I was lucky. It was as distant and unreachable as the far-off universe of Karazan.

It was a dream . . . and that's all it would ever be.

The truth was, I hadn't heard from them for weeks. I knew Q was busy putting the finishing touches to his latest computer game, the last in the Karazan series . . . and as for Hannah, she'd started school, written me one very careful letter with a picture of Tiger Lily at the bottom, and then gone quiet. Busy, learning lots. Making new friends. I was glad for them both – but that didn't stop me missing them, and dreaming . . .

As my thoughts drifted, the room lightened into grey pre-dawn. Gradually, the flickering shadows of the leaves faded and disappeared, till only the stark shadows of the bars remained.

Sometimes reality is all that's left.

REALITY

The first 'prospects' – as Mr Smigielski called them – were due to visit Highgate that afternoon, once we were all home from school.

Instead of the usual supervised playtime, we spent fifteen minutes racing round like whirlwinds tidying – not that there was much to tidy – and sprucing ourselves up. There was a weird atmosphere, like nothing I'd ever felt before at Highgate – excitement, tightly bottled up among us older kids, and a strange kind of shyness.

At 3:25 exactly, Mr Smigielski lined us all up in the rec room with our backs to the wall, in strict order of size. I was last in line. I was wearing the jeans and shirt I'd been allocated from the latest consignment of what Cookie called 'pre-loved clothing'. The jeans would probably have fitted me OK a couple of months back, but these days everything I put on seemed to end just above my ankle bones and wrists, leaving them sticking out in a knobbly, lost-looking way. The checked shirt felt tight over my shoulders. I hoped I wouldn't sneeze – the fabric was worn so thin that any sudden movement could easily make it split.

Hating myself for doing it, I'd washed my hair in the shower that morning. There was a tight knot of nerves right in the centre of my stomach, just under my ribs.

We were facing the clock on the rec room wall, every eye glued to the second hand as it jerked its slow way round. I glanced down the line of tidy heads, all neatly combed, some blond, some dark, some straight, some curly. They were exactly evenly spaced – Mr Smigielski had made sure of that. But to me, there was a gap in the line.

A gap where Weevil used to be.

It seemed everywhere I went were empty spaces where he would have been once, and never would be again. But I didn't think of him as Weevil now.

Staring up at the clock, I thought of Blue-bum. Where was he now? Had he gone back to the forest to join the other chatterbots? We'd all agreed that was most likely. Safely back in Quested Court, we'd had one of Jamie's 'secret meetings' and decided not to mention that Weevil had been left stranded in Karazan – or that he'd ever been there. As Rich said, no one except Q would ever have believed us . . . and what could be done about it? Blue-bum could hardly be brought back to Highgate to swing from the washing line while the rest of us kids were at school.

At first Matron had been suspected of being involved with his disappearance, but without any evidence no charges could be laid. As far as the rest of the world was concerned, Willie Weaver had simply vanished without a trace . . . and that's how we left it.

Now the minute hand of the clock jerked onto the 6 and the knot in my gut tightened. Chatterbot or not, I'd have changed places with Blue-bum in an instant – swapped the stuffy rec room and the ordeal that lay ahead for the freedom of the treetops in Karazan.

'And this,' said Mr Smigielski, as they finally reached me, 'is Adam Equinox.' He gave the couple a meaningful look. The husband was shorter than me, but built like a tank. He had a very red face with watery blue eyes and a square, jutting chin. His hair was short and curly like wool, and when he stuck out his hand to shake mine the back of it was covered in the same ginger hair. There was a funny smell about him I couldn't quite place.

I looked down at him and tried to smile, but my lips felt strangely stiff. I held out my hand – and instantly the bones were crunched in an agonising grip. Pain flared up my arm, and my eyes filled with tears. Shocked and confused, I blinked them angrily away. 'So,' he grunted, watching my face, 'not so tough now, eh?'

'Oh – is this the boy you were telling us about – the one who . . .' The wife's voice trailed away into silence. She was tiny – only up to his shoulder – and frail-looking as a bird. There was a kind of nervousness about the way she moved and spoke that reminded me of a bird too.

27

'Yes,' said Mr Smigielski coldly, 'this is the one.'

At last the man let go of my hand. It felt like it was broken. I wanted to rub it, but not in front of him.

'Now,' said Mr Smigielski smoothly, ushering them to the corner of the room, 'have you seen enough? Do you feel ready to make your decision?'

The husband turned to face us, arms folded, and glared down the line. 'I'm after a big lad,' he muttered, 'but not a load of trouble. Compost farming's no picnic, believe me.'

'They will all grow, remember,' murmured Mr Smigielski.

'It's very hard,' whispered the wife, glancing up at her husband apologetically. 'Remember the time we chose that puppy from the SPCA, dear? You just don't know how they'll turn out. And you can't help feeling rather sorry for them all, especially . . .' she glanced quickly at me, and then away again, 'the ones with . . . *no hope.*'

'Yes, unfortunately there are no guarantees,' said Mr Smigielski.

'You certainly don't want to choose one just because you feel sorry for it,' growled the husband. 'We did that with Baxter, and look where it got us. And you can't have a kid put down like you can a dog.'

'No,' she sighed, 'you're right, I'm afraid.'

'Well, come on! We need to make up our minds. I've a meeting at four thirty.'

'That one fourth from the end is a lovely-looking lad,' said the wife hesitantly. 'He's got a face like an angel, and that curly blond hair . . . just like in the photographs of you when you were a boy. Why, he could almost be our real son. Shall we take him?'

Luckily they weren't all like the ones who took Geoffrey. There was the elderly couple who broke down in tears when they saw Moira, because she reminded them so much of their own daughter, dead for twenty years.

And there was the librarian, a single lady 'or old maid, to be perfectly blunt about it,' she told us all crisply, but with a twinkle in her eye. She asked Mr Smigielski to leave her alone with us, and talked to each one of us in turn. When she came to little Frankie, the kid with the real bad stammer, she crouched right down to his level before she spoke. 'And what is your name, dear?' she asked gently.

He gulped – a strangled, choking sound. His huge eyes stared desperately from his thin face. It was a desperation I understood. Frankie, like me, was 'marginal'.

'F-f-f-f-f-f-' he stuttered.

She looked deep into his pleading eyes . . . and then she reached out both arms and drew him close. 'Don't worry, little one,' she whispered. 'You've told me all I need to know. Come with me.'

And as she led him to the door, there was a look on Frankie's face I'd never seen in all my years at Highgate.

★

29

A month later, at the end of the school term, I was the only one left. Even Cookie had gone, packing her few possessions into a battered suitcase and giving me a squashy hug that smelled of dough. 'You be a good boy, Adam,' she told me in a fierce whisper. 'You're bigger than all of this. Everything will come right for you, you'll see.' I hugged her back. I wished I didn't ever have to let go. Most of all, I wished it was true.

Mr Smigielski watched silently from the door. He'd be driving Cookie to the bus terminus to catch the coach to her new position, at a girls' reformatory school.

I watched Mr Smigielski's sleek black car purr away down the driveway, Cookie's face peering back at me through the window, and felt as if I was losing the last friend I had in the world.

That evening at dinnertime there was only Mr Smigielski and me. The house felt huge, echoing, and empty as a tomb.

Every day of my life the dinner bell had rung to summon us kids to the dining room. Today, no bell rang. At six thirty, my stomach growling with hunger, I hovered near the door, wondering what to do. Should I go in? Who would make dinner with Cookie gone? Would there be dinner at all?

At last I summoned up the courage to peek round the door. There, at the head of one of the long wooden tables, sat Mr Smigielski in his black suit. He had a clean napkin tucked under his Adam's apple. There was a tray on the table in front of him, with three or four of the chipped white institution dishes set out on it.

He looked up and saw me, but his expression didn't change. He patted his lips with the napkin. 'Ah, Adam,' he said. 'Come in.'

Awkwardly, I shuffled forward.

'Sit down.' I pulled out a chair and sat, trying to see what was in the dishes without seeming to look. 'Perhaps you would care to join me in a little dinner.'

'Yeah! Thanks, that'd be great!' It was the last thing I'd been expecting.

He gestured to the dishes. 'My diet is somewhat bland, I fear. I suffer from a peptic ulcer, and am obliged to avoid red meat and other foods which might exacerbate the ailment.' So it wasn't steak and chips. Well, my nose had told me that before I even walked in the door.

'I can offer you a little steamed fish . . .' He gestured to one of the plates. 'Little' was right – a dry-looking piece of plain white fish the size of a playing card, with a dismal heap of grey-green stuff beside it in a small puddle of water. '. . . with spinach.' He indicated a side plate. 'A boiled potato.' He was right, there was – one. 'A portion of brown rice, moistened with organic yoghurt.' He pointed to something that looked like cat-sick in a cereal bowl. 'A small bowl of junket. Or a well-ripened banana.'

I hesitated. None of it looked great, especially the junket, which I'd never even heard of. It looked like white jelly – made from milk, maybe? I couldn't begin to guess how it would taste. One thing was for sure: that meal was only enough for one person – at a push. 'I dunno,' I mumbled, feeling myself flush. Truth was, I could have hoovered up the lot in less than a minute – even the cat-sick and the junket. 'I'd hate to take any of your meal . . .'

'Very well,' he said. 'In that case, if you will excuse me . . .'

He forked up a few grains of cat-sick and slid it into his mouth, chewing rapidly with a little clicking sound.

'Does that mean . . . I can go?'

The peach stone bobbed, and he gave his lips another pat with the napkin. 'In a moment. First, there is the matter of your future to discuss.

'I have contacted Rippingale Hall and made arrangements for your transfer there. There is a train tomorrow afternoon. You will be on it.'

'*Tomorrow?*' I gawked at him. 'But . . . what will happen about school? My . . . my friends, and . . .'

'Fortunately the school term ends tomorrow. There will be ample time to make alternative arrangements regarding your education. And as for friends . . . I was not aware that you had any.'

I thought of Cameron. I hadn't told him any of this. I was too ashamed . . . and too afraid he might think I was hoping . . .

'Can I go to school tomorrow?' I asked. Suddenly I desperately wanted to talk to Cam one more time, even if it was just to say goodbye. 'For the last day? *Please?*'

'The issue is not whether you *can* go; it is whether you *may*.' Mr Smigielski peeled his banana, considering. 'I see no reason why you should not,' he pronounced at last. 'Education is, after all, a precious jewel that should be prized above all others.

'Perhaps there is hope for you after all, Adam Equinox.'

AN UNEXPECTED
DEVELOPMENT

'But ... where *is* this Rippingale Hall?' Cameron peered at me through his thick specs, his forehead creased with worry.

'He didn't say. A long way from here. That's all I know.'

'And you're going *today*? Right *now*?'

I nodded miserably.

'I don't believe it. People can't *do* stuff like that! There must be laws against it. Maybe I could ask my dad . . .' Cam was digging in his backpack. School was over for the term – for me, it was over forever. For once the long hours had flown by with the swiftness of seconds; the chattering crowd outside the gate had evaporated around us while I mumbled my startling news to Cameron . . . and now we were the only ones left. 'Tell you what – we'll make a list . . .'

Old Cam and his lists. He didn't realise there were some problems no list in the world would ever solve. I put my hand on his arm. 'No, Cam,' I told him as gently as I could. 'That won't help this time. Instead, write down your address for me. Not your e-mail one

– I don't think there'll be a computer where I'm going. Your postal address. Somehow, sometime, I'll write to you –' I felt myself blush – 'but just don't expect miracles, OK?'

He looked at me and shook his head. His specs were misted over, so I couldn't see the expression in his eyes. Then he scribbled on the piece of paper and pressed it into my hand. 'I still don't believe this is happening,' he muttered.

I opened my mouth to say goodbye, but suddenly I knew I couldn't do it. My throat had got itself clogged up, and nothing – not even the tiniest word – was going to be able to fit through. Instead, I put my hand on his skinny shoulder and gave it a quick squeeze.

Then I turned and headed away up the hill towards Highgate for the very last time.

My feet crunched up the gravel drive. I climbed the red concrete steps to the entrance porch, same as I'd done a thousand times before. I stopped on the second step, staring down at the five long, parallel runnels that ran from one end of each step to the other, as if a giant had taken a massive fork and drawn it across when the concrete was wet. I looked at the places on the edge where the smooth red surface had chipped away to leave crescents of rough grey cement. I'd never consciously noticed them before, but now I realised they were as familiar to me as my own face in the mirror.

I walked through the front door and felt the cool

darkness settle round me. It smelled different: of emptiness, and silence. I walked through to the dining hall to put my lunch box on the servery, same as I always did – though there was no point now. And that's when I realised.

The long tables were all gone. The chairs, with their wooden seats polished smooth by wriggling bottoms . . . my own bottom, right from when I'd been so small I could only just peek over the table-top, till now. The built-in servery was still there; but the kitchen beyond it was empty, with greasy dents on the lino where the appliances and cupboards had stood.

I walked slowly down the passage to the rec room, knowing what I would find. Pushed the door open, hearing it creak in the silence. Gone – everything was gone. The grey plastic chairs, the computer, my favourite chair with the broken spring, the television, the rickety bookcase in the corner . . . even the dusty games and the puzzles with half the pieces missing that no one had played with for years. There were dusty patches on the threadbare carpet where the things had once stood. Other than that, they might never have existed. The removal firm must have come while I was at school and taken everything away.

Everything?

I hurried back down the passage to the boys' dorm. The door was closed. I reached out a hand, grasped the doorknob. Hesitated, almost afraid of what I would see. Swung the door open.

The beds were gone – all of them. The metal

36

bedside cabinets, the lockers – gone. The room looked way bigger than it used to do.

There by the far wall, where my bed used to be, was a small, pathetic pile of stuff. I knelt down and checked it through. My few clothes were there, even the special ones I'd been given by Q. Still folded neatly, arranged in a tidy pile. My shawl was there, rolled the way I'd left it. I undid it and checked. Felt my heart do an almost painful forward roll of relief. My penny whistle was safe inside.

But my *Bible* – my *Bible* was gone. And inside it . . .

I stared wildly round, hoping it might be lying somewhere, hidden . . .

But there was nowhere for it to hide.

Only Mr Smigielski, standing silently at the door, watching me.

'P-please, Mr Smeegulski,' I stammered, still kneeling on the floor clutching my shawl, 'my *Bible* – where's my *Bible*?'

He gave a small frown. 'Technically, Adam, any items that may have been assigned to you on your arrival remain the property of Highgate. The other children may well have taken their *Bibles* with them when they left – but whether they were within their rights to do so is debatable. What you term "your" *Bible* has been sent to Central City Auctions with the rest of the oddments as a job lot. We may not receive much for it, alas, but . . .'

'But . . . but . . . *there was something of mine in it!*'

He shrugged, the merest twitch of the narrow

shoulders beneath the black cloth of his jacket. 'Too late, I fear. Such childish trifles can hardly be important to you now.'

I stared up at him, hollow with disbelief. The newspaper clipping – the only remaining link to my lost parents – was gone.

Automatically, as stiffly as a robot, I packed my things away into my school bag. They fitted easily. I stumbled to my feet. My legs felt prickly and wooden, as if they'd gone to sleep.

'Well,' I said dully, 'I guess that's it then. I'm ready to go.'

'Excellent.' Mr Smigielski rubbed his hands together. For him, the job was nearly done. The dry skin of his palms made a rustling, papery sound in the stillness of the dorm.

'There is one thing, however. A slight change of plan. What one might term . . . an unexpected development. While you were at school, I received a telephone call – quite out of the blue, one might say. It was from a person who it appears wishes to foster you, against all probability. Apparently they know you well, and have an interest in your welfare. You will be collected shortly – in approximately fifteen minutes, I believe,' he continued, consulting his watch.

'Your future home will be a small town by the name of . . . Winterton.'

OUT OF THE BLUE

Winterton – Quested Court – *Q!*

I gaped at Mr Smigielski, hardly daring to believe it was true. 'Winterton?' I croaked. 'Truly? Are you . . . are you absolutely sure?'

His lips twitched into a ghost of a smile. 'Indeed I am. Do you wish to know the name of your bene-factor?'

I shook my head, grinning up at him from under my thatch of hair. 'You don't need to tell me,' I told him. 'I already know.'

I sat on the top step with the afternoon sun baking hot patches on the knees of my jeans, and waited.

Sure enough, almost exactly a quarter of an hour later I heard a car engine approaching up the hill, and the crunch of tyres turning into the driveway. But it wasn't the big forest-green four-by-four I'd been expecting – instead, a low-slung black sports car swept through the open gate. The door opened and a slim figure unfolded itself, reaching back in for a crocodile-skin handbag, and closing the door again with a decisive *click*. I felt a pang of disappointment. I'd hoped Q would fetch me himself – or at worst, send Shaw. But here was Usherwood, the only person at Quested Court I didn't entirely trust . . . or even very much like. Watching her walk towards me across the gravel with her usual cool, watchful expression, her sleek hair shining like starling feathers in the sunlight, I thought again how much she reminded me of a bird of prey.

She stopped at the foot of the steps and looked at me with a strange little crooked smile, as if she was waiting for something. Hastily, I scrambled to my feet. I knew what she must be thinking: that it was high time I learned some manners. I'd need them, where I was going! I wiped my hand on the seat of my jeans and held it out to her. 'Hi, Ms Usherwood,' I mumbled.

She took my big mitt in the tips of her fingers and held it for a second. Her skin felt cool and smooth. She was still looking up at me like she somehow expected me to say something more. I shuffled my feet awkwardly, racking my brains. What was she waiting for? Yeah, right! 'Uh . . . thanks – thanks for coming to get me,' I muttered.

'It's a pleasure,' she said formally, with a tilt of her head and a lift of one eyebrow, and that same odd, unsettling smile. I felt myself squirm. Life at Quested Court was going to have its tough patches with old Usherwood around – especially if she'd decided to take sole responsibility for knocking off my rough corners and polishing me up. Still, I grinned to myself, Quested Court was a big place; she'd be easy enough to avoid.

'Is that all the luggage you have?' she was asking. 'In that case put it in the car, and wait there while I complete a few formalities.'

I slouched down the steps, but her voice brought me up short. 'Adam . . . *after* you have said your farewells, of course.'

Sure enough, there in the doorway stood old Mr S, with his usual knack of materialising out of nowhere. So up the steps I went again, holding out a sweaty paw. 'Goodbye, Mr Shmuggleski,' I mumbled, shooting a wary glance at the Usherwood. 'Uh . . . thanks . . . I guess.'

He gave a frosty smile, and tweaked the tips of my fingers briefly as if he was afraid I might contaminate him. 'Goodbye, Adam.' Then he turned to Ms Usherwood. 'And now, madam, if you could accompany me inside for a moment . . .'

Together, they disappeared into the darkness of the hallway.

With a sigh of relief, I shouldered my bag and mooched over to the car. Was about to lower myself in, when I had a sudden thought. I straightened and looked over at the big white house, cool and shuttered-looking in the sunshine. Suddenly it looked lonely, and somehow sad. There was no Usherwood to remind me . . . but this time I didn't need to be told. *Goodbye, Highgate*, I said in my mind. *And thank you . . . for everything*.

But the big old house didn't say a word.

From the beginning, it looked as if the trip to Quested Court was going to be a long one. The little car was nippy and fast, and Ms Usherwood drove with smooth confidence, keeping the needle dead on the speed limit all the way – not a hair over, not a hair under.

But the conversation didn't exactly flow.

Once we'd navigated the various twists and turns and were safely on the northern motorway, I figured I'd better start the ball rolling. After all, she'd driven for five hours or so to fetch me, and I didn't want to seem ungrateful. 'So,' I said chattily, squirming in the seat to get comfortable, 'Q – I guess he's real busy, then?'

'Q?' goes Usherwood, like she'd never even heard of him . . . or as if her mind had been miles away. 'Yes, he certainly is.'

So I was right – that was why he hadn't come himself.

'With the new game . . . the last one, huh?' I persevered.

She nodded briefly, her eyes on the road ahead. 'Yes.'

I gave an inward sigh. She sure was hard work! Still, I figured it was only polite to keep trying. 'And Hannah,' I tried again. 'How's old Hannah?'

Usherwood's lips tightened slightly. 'She is well.'

I opened my mouth to ask after Tiger Lily, but then I noticed the tiny frown on Usherwood's smooth forehead, and thought better of it. She seemed to have a lot on her mind – or maybe she had her nose out of joint about having to trail all the way to Redcliff and back.

As for me . . . I'd hardly slept the night before, and there was something soothing and hypnotic about the hum of the tyres on the tarmac, and the endless ribbon of road unravelling in front of us. I snuggled deeper into the soft leather, rested my head back and closed my eyes. It was a new experience to let my thoughts drift into dreams knowing that when I woke up, they'd all be coming true.

When at last I surfaced from sleep it was completely dark – way too dark to see where we were. At some stage Ms Usherwood must have turned on the car radio; some kind of fuddy-duddy classical music was playing softly. I wondered how much further there was to go – by now we must be nearly there! I opened my mouth to ask, but the question turned into a ginormous yawn.

Just as I was in the middle of it, staring blearily through the windscreen at the pale wash of the head-lights in the rushing darkness, I saw something that made me sit bolt upright and snap my mouth shut so quickly I nearly dislocated my jaw. We *were* almost there! The headlights picked out a sign up ahead – the same one I'd shone my torch on in the pouring rain the first time I'd been to Quested Court; the same one I'd roared past with Q the second time, hardly even noticing it. *Winterton 5, Hamley 45* – and an arrow pointing off to the left, in the direction of Quested Court.

And Usherwood had zoomed right past it without even slowing down!

'Hey!' I yelped. 'You've missed the turnoff!'

But she didn't even so much as touch the brake; just slid me a sidelong glance and a small smile. 'Oh, you're awake. Good sleep, Adam?'

'*Ms Usherwood . . .*'

'Don't you think you might consider calling me Veronica, Adam?'

Veronica? Was she crazy? Why would I want to do that? But, 'Yeah, whatever,' I gabbled. 'The thing is, Ms . . . Vermrrrr –' I couldn't bring myself to say it – '*you've gone right past*!'

'Past what?' She looked over at me with a slight frown.

'Past the road to Quested Court! I saw the sign way back there!'

'We're not going to Quested Court, Adam,' she said, in the same kind of slow, extra-patient voice the school careers dude had used to explain about my learning problem. 'Not tonight.'

'But . . . what's the point of stopping off some-where tonight when we're so close? And Q –' suddenly I felt the prickle of tears at the back of my eyes –

'Q and Hannah – they'll be expecting me!'

At last the car slowed, pulling over onto the hard shoulder and coming to a standstill. I peered over my shoulder to check there was nothing coming up behind, so it was safe to turn. We'd gone way past the sign; I couldn't even see it back there in the darkness. 'It's all clear,' I told her. 'Right back as far as I can see.'

But instead of flipping a U-turn she switched the engine off. The music droned softly on in the sudden silence. The car was dark, but not too dark for me to see her face. It had a strange expression on it. For a crazy second I wondered if she was kidnapping me . . . or planning to murder me, there in the middle of nowhere. But then she spoke . . . and what she said was worse than murder. Way worse.

'Adam . . . what did Mr Smigielski tell you, back at Highgate?'

'That – that I was coming to Winterton, of course,' I stammered, 'and that –' I felt myself flush in the darkness, shy to be saying the words out loud for the first time – 'that Q was . . . adopting me.'

Her next words were very, very gentle – and so kind she didn't sound like Usherwood at all. 'Oh, Adam. Was that what Mr Smigielski said . . . or what *you* heard?

'It isn't Q who's adopting you.

'It's me.'

A ROOM OF MY OWN

For what seemed an eternity I sat there paralysed, hearing her words echo over and over in my mind: '*It's me . . . me . . . me . . . me . . . me . . .*' But it was as if they were in some weird language I didn't understand.

From somewhere far away came the tiny, metallic ticking of the engine cooling in the night air.

Then at last the meaning of what she'd said slammed into my gut like a fist.

Blindly, desperately, I fumbled for the door handle; grabbed it and yanked it open. Stumbled out of the car, tripping over my own feet and crashing to my knees in the rough grass by the side of the road. I crawled frantically away from the car in the direction of the signboard, the direction of Q . . .

Struggled to my feet, ran a few staggering steps . . . then slowed and stopped.

Finally, standing there in the darkness, I realised the truth. *It wasn't Q. It never had been. There was no point running to Q. He didn't want me. He never had.*

'Adam.' Usherwood's voice came from behind me,

near the car. 'Adam – I'm sorry. I know how you feel about Q. He's an exceptional man. But he lives in a world of his own – you know that. He has a brilliant mind; but like most geniuses, when it comes to responsibility, to practical things . . .'

Awkwardly, as if I was in a dream, I shambled round to face her. She'd left the car lights on. They stretched away into the distance, lighting up the road ahead until at last they were lost in the darkness.

Usherwood was standing between me and the car, slim and straight, silhouetted against the glare of the headlights.

'Why?' I croaked. And then again, louder: '*Why? Just tell me that. I don't understand. Why would you want to adopt me . . . you*, of all people?'

I couldn't see her face. After a long pause she answered me, her voice flat and unemotional. 'Is it so strange that I might want a child?' The words reminded me of Mr Smigielski's, what seemed like a lifetime ago. *I am constantly astonished by how many people long for a child.*

But *Usherwood*?

'Let's just say it has to do with something that lies in the past, Adam. Something that happened a long, long time ago. We'll leave it at that – for the moment at least.'

Staring at her, trying to make sense of her words, I realised I was shivering in my thin shirt.

'You're cold. Get in the car again; we'll go home and get you settled in. Things will look better in the morning. Apart from anything else . . .' I thought I could hear a hint of a wry smile in her voice, 'we'll be paying a visit to your precious Q. I've persuaded him to hold a small pre-release press conference for the new game . . . but I'll tell you more about that tomorrow.'

We drove the rest of the way in silence. I was numb with disbelief. It felt like my brain had completely stopped working . . . and deep down I was in no hurry for it to start again. The prospect of spending the next few years at Rippingale Hall had been bad enough; but the thought of a future stretching endlessly ahead under Usherwood's icy scrutiny was almost worse.

Less than five minutes later we pulled into a narrow driveway and stopped outside a tumbledown cottage. Someone – Usherwood, presumably – had left a light on downstairs, and it shone through the window onto an overgrown garden. 'I thought you lived at Quested Court,' I muttered, opening my door and clambering reluctantly out.

'I did, until a few days ago.' She didn't say so, but that stark statement made it obvious that Usherwood had moved because . . . well, because of me. I guessed you couldn't really shift a lanky thirteen-year-old into your employer's house, even if it was one the size of Quested Court. But . . .

'Does he know – about me, I mean?'

'Adam,' said Usherwood with exaggerated patience, 'Q has been working twenty hours a day for the past few months. He barely knows his own name at present. Yes, I told him what I was planning, and yes, I told him I was moving out – but for all the attention he paid, I might as well have told the cat. Frankly, I doubt he's even noticed my absence. Now: would you like some supper?'

I shook my head. I'd had nothing to eat since sharing Cam's lunch at school, but I felt as if I'd never be hungry again. All I wanted was to be alone – and think.

She unlocked the front door and led the way into a small hallway. Doors led off to the left and right, but Usherwood ignored them, heading straight upstairs. 'This will be your bedroom,' she announced, opening a door on the landing. 'There's only one bathroom, I'm afraid. My room is there –' she indicated a door further along the passage – 'and there's a lounge and kitchen downstairs. Breakfast will be at eight sharp. Sleep well.'

Automatically I pushed the door open and went in. The first flicker of feeling made its way through my numbness, a tiny glimmer of light in the dark. *A room of my own.* I fumbled for the light switch and turned it on.

The small room was bright and cheerful, and every-thing in it was squeaky-new. I glanced round, taking in the single bed with its squashy-looking patchwork cover and fat feather pillow, a wooden desk, a book-case crammed with an assortment of kids' books.

I tossed my bag onto the bed, walked over to the

window and pulled the curtain open. It looked out over the back garden – a patch of lawn surrounded by overgrown flowerbeds, with a dark hedgerow on the far side. Beyond that was the black emptiness of fields. Somewhere far away I heard the hoarse bleat of a sheep calling to its lamb. Apart from that, there was silence.

It was all way weird. Why would Usherwood want a kid – especially a kid like me? I didn't know much about mothers, but it seemed to me that Ms Usherwood had about as much maternal instinct as a rattlesnake. *'Is it so strange that I might want a child?'* she'd asked. The short answer to that was: 'Yes.'

Usherwood didn't like me – I was under no illusions about that. Yet right from the beginning there'd been something about the way she'd looked at me – as if I was a complicated sum, and she was trying to figure me out.

I shrugged. The bottom line was, I didn't like her either, and I didn't trust her one bit. I was more and more certain it had been Usherwood who'd snooped in my room at Quested Court that night long ago – though what she'd been looking for, I couldn't begin to imagine.

Frowning at the empty doorway, I noticed the key in the lock – and at long last I managed a wry grin. What the heck – for the first time in my life I had a room of my own, and it was cool. I was better off than I would have been at Rippingale Hall, that was for sure. No matter how closely old Usherwood watched me, I'd watch her closer still. After all, I'd had thirteen years of intensive training from the best possible teacher: Matron.

I padded across the floor and turned the key. Then I stripped to my boxers, tucked my shawl into bed, slid in beside it and snuggled down, my fingers feeling for the familiar contours of my ring.

I turned off the bedside light, slipped my thumb into my mouth, and reached for my shawl. The warmth and silence of the snug little room wrapped themselves round me like a cocoon. Staring up at the silvery wash of moonlight on the sloping ceiling, a thought drifted into my mind: *I could get used to this . . .*

But I didn't get the chance.

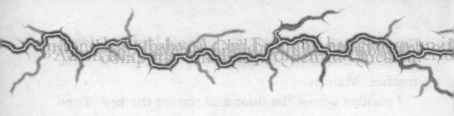

THE FINAL GAME

I was woken by the racket of a zillion birds chirruping and squabbling outside the window. Cautiously, I unlocked the door and peeked out. All clear. I hopped into the shower, tugged my comb through my hair and threw on the jeans and T-shirt Q had given me, trying to forget it was Usherwood who'd actually chosen them.

I had no idea what the time was, but the shadows in the garden were long, and there was dew sparkling on the grass. Feeling shy and awkward, a twist of nerves tugging at my gut, I tiptoed downstairs.

One of the doors was open a crack, and I could hear a radio playing quietly behind it, tuned to some kind of news programme.

Hesitantly, I pushed the door open. Usherwood was sitting at a kitchen table set for two, drinking coffee. She looked at her watch. 'Five minutes late,' she remarked. 'Sit down and help yourself to muesli and a slice of toast – and hurry up. We need to be off in twenty minutes – the press is arriving at ten o'clock, and there's a great deal to do before then. There'll be television coverage too, on the evening news.'

I slid onto the empty chair and reached for the cereal packet, wondering how much it was polite to take. I was starving. 'What's happening, exactly?' I risked asking.

'Today is the final deadline for the pilot copy of the last game in the Karazan series,' Usherwood rattled off, very much in business mode. 'I'm assuming Q has finally finished it – he swore he was on track when I last saw him. Among other things, we'll be announcing the title, which until now has been strictly embargoed.' She shot me a glance. 'Top secret, in your terms, Adam. In addition, there'll be a set-up of a group of children loading the game for the very first time – the opening screen, and a glimpse of the video prelims. All fairly standard marketing procedure – but in the case of this particular game, the level of public interest will be huge.'

She was firing on all cylinders, that much was clear. Most of what she was going on about went straight over my head – but one thing did stick. 'A group of children?' I asked, through a mouthful of what tasted like horse food. 'What children?'

'Don't talk with your mouth full, Adam. I would expect better manners of someone with an orphanage upbringing. Never mind – I'll soon get you into shape. Once the launch is over we'll get that skin seen to – I have an excellent specialist. It's all about toxins. Yes, that's a top priority – along with a decent haircut and intensive remedial tuition throughout the holidays.

A learning disability is sheer self-indulgence, in my view.' She frowned at me. 'You should drink a minimum of eight glasses of water a day, you know. And now, if you will excuse me, I have a number of matters to attend to before we leave. Kindly clear the table and load your plate into the dishwasher when you've finished, and meet me outside in –' she consulted her watch – 'fifteen minutes – by which time I expect you to have made your bed and tidied your room. And bring down the car keys – they're on my dressing table.'

I swallowed, feeling the mouthful of oats and bran grinding its slow way down my throat like sandpaper. 'Ms . . . Vrrrmph,' I tried again, hoping the bits still stuck between my teeth didn't count as a full mouth, 'what children?'

She paused for a moment on her way to the door, glancing back impatiently over her shoulder. 'The others, of course: Richard, James, Kenta and Genevieve.'

I gobbled the rest of my breakfast and stashed the plate and spoon in the dishwasher, then raced upstairs and made my bed. There was nothing in my room to tidy, but I put my shawl and penny whistle into my backpack along with a sweatshirt, and slung it over my shoulder. Then, warily, I padded down the passage to Usherwood's room. The door was ajar. I knocked softly before easing it open, though I could hear her rattling round downstairs.

Although I'd been told to come, I had an

uncomfortable feeling of trespassing. I headed straight over to what I guessed must be the dresser – a dark wood chest of drawers with a mirror over it – and scanned the surface for the keys. It was cluttered with stuff – a hairbrush, a perfume bottle I guessed was responsible for the faint musky fragrance that hung in the air, a jumble of bottles and jars. I grinned to myself, remembering that comment about my table manners. Matron would have had something to say about the dusting of powder covering the polished surface, never mind the mess. Cleanser, toner, moisturiser, concealing cream ... *Shoot*, I thought, *it's good to be a guy* ... Then I spotted the keys behind a pink bottle of something called 'foundation' and was out of there, closing the door thankfully behind me.

The little black sports car drew up outside Quested Court in a spray of gravel; Usherwood leapt out and bustled up the steps and through the big arched door without a backward glance.

I unfolded myself from the passenger seat and followed, more hesitantly. The first time I'd been here I'd felt like an interloper; the second time, like a guest of honour. This time I didn't have a clue how to feel, what was expected of me, or where I fitted in.

I paused outside the door, which had swung almost closed. Raised my hand to the big brass knocker, wondering if I should knock or march straight in like Usherwood had done.

Before I could make up my mind the door was flung

open and there was Q. His few wispy tendrils of gingery hair sprung up from his freckled head like corkscrews, and his glasses sat askew on his knobbly nose. He was even thinner than I remembered, and more like a scarecrow than ever. He was wearing corduroy trousers, a striped pyjama top, and a tie with an egg stain on it. A battered sheepskin slipper was on one foot, and a sock with a hole in the toe on the other.

He was more excited than I'd ever seen him. 'Adam!' he cried, holding out his arms. 'My dear, dear boy! What's all this Usherwood is telling me – and never a word to anyone! All most odd . . . but just imagine – it's finished! Yes, in the early hours of this morning – my *magnus opus* – my greatest game yet! And do you know, my boy, it virtually wrote itself? Yes, finished at last . . . and you dear children here to help celebrate! Come in, come in . . . come and join us for some supper before Usherwood's press vultures descend!'

'Not supper, Q – breakfast.' There was Hannah, her face set in a severe frown. I grinned at her, my heart lifting. She was only five years old, but sometimes you'd have thought old Hannah was the first female dictator of the world. 'You come back into the dining room right now and eat something! You've buttered your bacon and put tomato sauce on your toast – and you've poured coffee on your cereal *again*!' Suddenly her eyes widened in alarm. 'Look out, everyone!' she squawked. Something small and furry and fast as a rocket shot out from nowhere, zipped between my legs, and zoomed through the library door, followed seconds later by a super-charged cream-coloured streak that disappeared after it like a heat-seeking missile. 'That's Bluebell and Tiger Lily, playing tag again,' Hannah announced disapprovingly. 'I wouldn't play if *I* was Bluebell, 'cos Tiger Lily never lets her win.'

And at last she shot me her special zillion-dollar grin. 'Hi, Adam. Thank goodness you're here. Boy, do we need you!'

It was great to see the others again, but I hardly had time for more than a grin for the girls and a high five and sweaty handshake for Rich and Jamie before we were set to work, the girls in the kitchen helping Nanny, us boys rearranging the computer room for the TV shoot. Shaw was in charge; he gave me a shrewd look and a brief 'Adam, good ter see yer.' But for once I had a feeling I could tell what was behind his broad, impassive face: there was more he wanted to say. I was right. It wasn't long before he took me aside, supposedly to help carry some water jugs and bowls of peppermints into the library for the press conference.

'So, Adam,' he rumbled, 'wot's all this about Usherwood, then?'

I shrugged awkwardly, shuffling my feet. 'I dunno,' I mumbled. 'It's weird. She's . . . fostering me or something, I guess.'

'That's wot I 'eard,' said Shaw grimly. 'Though not

from '*er*, mind. Odd, ain't it? 'Oo'd 'ave thought Usherwood was the broody type? Now listen ter me, Adam: you 'ave any problems – any worries at all, mind – and you come straight ter me. Right?'

I looked up into his deep-set dark eyes and nodded. 'Yeah,' I told him. 'I will. But don't worry, Shaw – I'm sure Ms Usherwood means well . . .' But even I could hear the doubt in my voice. Shaw shook his big head dubiously, and laid a heavy hand on my shoulder for a moment.

Then there was the sound of an engine outside, and car doors slamming. The press had descended – and from then on it was all action.

Q reappeared, shepherded by Usherwood, dressed to the nines in a starched white shirt, shiny-looking black suit and black bow tie. He looked miserably uncomfortable, and kept tugging at the tie – which was already creeping round so the bow was under his ear – and fiddling unhappily with his specs, which for once were sparkling clean.

What seemed like a battalion of men and women with tape recorders, microphones and notepads disappeared behind the library door, which was firmly shut. 'The press conference will take place first,' Usherwood had informed us earlier, 'and your presence is not required. You will be involved in the television segment, however – there'll be a brief interview with Q, and then a sequence of shots involving all or some of you in front of the computer. Just do as you're told and don't fidget.'

We waited in a nervous huddle by my desk in the computer room. All the other tables had been moved over to the sides of the room to make space for what Usherwood mysteriously called 'the equipment'.

'I've never been on TV before,' admitted Rich with a bashful grin. 'I hope we don't have to say anything.'

'Don't worry, Rich – just be natural,' advised Jamie, who was looking anything but natural in a pale grey suit and tie. 'I've been on TV heaps of times – well, once. They were interviewing kids from my school about our views on the future of education –'

'Shhhh, Jamie – here they come!' hissed Gen, with a little squiggle of excitement. Into the room marched Usherwood, Q trailing reluctantly behind her with a strange man in smart grey slacks, a jacket and a tie.

'The reporter,' Jamie whispered. Behind them came Shaw and a scruffy-looking guy in jeans, hiking boots and a T-shirt, both almost hidden under a mountain of equipment. 'That's the cameraman,' breathed Jamie reverently. 'Bet you can't guess how much one of those cameras costs! It –'

But we never got to find out, because the cameraman gave us a grin and a wink and said cheerfully, 'So: you kids are the *real* stars of the show, eh? Come on over here and give me a hand with these lights!'

As I helped the cameraman – whose name was Carl – plug in the two tall free-standing lights and position them, I listened with half an ear to the reporter briefing Q. 'I'll start off by setting the scene, Mr Quested – then we'll switch to you, and I'll run through some basic questions – the title of the game; as much as you're prepared to say about the content; how long it took you to write; any problems along the way . . . nothing tricky. When we edit later on back at the studio, we'll intersperse the interview sequence with shots of the children turning on the computer and loading the game for the first time . . . the aim is to build up a story in pictures. Carl will want to film four or five shots of the same bit of action from different perspectives . . . but he'll have a chat to the kids about that shortly. Now, are we ready?'

Q nodded unhappily, tugging at his tie. Rich lowered himself back-to-front on my computer chair to watch the fun, grinning broadly. The chair gave a loud squeak as he settled more comfortably, and Usherwood glared at him. 'There's no need for you children to be here,' she said crisply. 'Q will feel more at ease without an audience, I'm sure. Out you go!'

'Oh, but Usherwood –' began Gen pleadingly.

'*Ms* Usherwood to you, Genevieve,' she snapped, holding the door open. I sighed and led the way out into the passage. Even a short time in the company of my newly appointed guardian had taught me that arguing would be a waste of breath.

As I'd expected, we couldn't hear a thing through the thick wooden door. 'I've been *dying* to find out about that new game,' Jamie complained. 'And now I guess we'll have to wait till the news tonight, just like everyone else! It doesn't seem fair, when we're the ones who've actually been to Karazan, and we're right on the spot, here at Quested Court –'

The door popped open and Carl the cameraman poked his head round. 'OK, kids,' he said cheerily. 'That was short and sweet. You're up next. Let's hope we can pad it out a bit with some really exciting visuals. Now,' he went on, putting his hands on his hips and inspecting us with a mock frown, 'we'll need a driver for the computer. Who's volunteering to be the one to press the magic button?'

'I will!' said Jamie instantly, raising a pudgy hand. 'I've got the most experience – I've been on TV before. And I don't mind saying a few words, if you'd –'

'Hmmm ... I think not, young man; we'll use you to add a bit of ... background interest.' His cell-phone rang, and he answered it with an apologetic smile. 'Yeah, all under way. Right on schedule. No problems.' The phone went back into his pocket; then: 'You.' To my horror he pointed decisively at me. 'You'll do just fine. Sit down in the chair and pull it up in front of the box. That's the ticket. Now: I want the rest of you grouped round – what's your name, son?'

'Adam,' I muttered reluctantly.

'Grouped round Adam, as if he's been given the game for his birthday and you're all his mates, just dying to watch him open it for the first time. Ms Usherwood –' she hurried forward – 'pass over the cover of the game, would you? I'll set it up beside the

61

computer; we'll start with a close-up of it, then pull focus to a wide shot; then another close-up of Adam's hands on the keyboard . . .'

His voice rattled on, but I didn't hear a word. I was staring at the shiny cardboard sleeve covering the box of Q's new computer game. I'd seen the covers of the other five games, and they were all super-cool – they had a kind of magnetism that would make them stand out anywhere, even in a shop crammed full of computer games. This one was even more awesome than the others . . . but it had an ominous, sinister quality that filled me with a sickening sense of foreboding.

In the background was a towering, many-turreted castle set high on a mountain peak. Not Shakesh – I saw that at once. While Shakesh had been squat and brooding, this castle's turrets were like long, skeletal fingers clutching at the sky . . . a sky bulbous with purple clouds like tumorous growths, shot through with vicious forks of jagged lightning.

Behind the castle, so huge it almost filled the sky, was a massive face. It was faint and shadowy, like a face in a dream. You didn't even see it at first . . . but once you had, you couldn't see anything else. The skin had the grey pallor of a corpse, the dark hair under the twisted crown blending into the gloom of the surrounding sky. The mouth was thin and cruel. And the eyes . . . the eyes were staring and bloodshot, and seemed to be boring straight into my soul. I barely saw the five small figures in the foreground of the picture, silhouetted against the menacing sky;

barely saw the name of the game, emblazoned in bold scarlet letters over the dark plain at the foot of the mountain:

POWER QUEST TO KARAZAN

My whole being was focused on that shadowy face; those hungry, searching eyes.

Incredibly – impossibly – it was the face of King Karazeel.

A MESSAGE FROM
ANOTHER WORLD

I t couldn't be.

I knew that the whole history of Karazan –
King Zane and Queen Zaronel and evil King
Karazeel, and a past that stretched back thousands
of years before them – was part of what Q called
'spontaneous evolution', a process I sensed even Q
didn't fully understand. Basically, it meant that
Karazan had developed into a real world, with heaps
of stuff in it even Q didn't know about. Q hadn't
invented King Karazeel: he'd simply happened, in the
separate dimension that was Karazan. And Q hadn't
ever been to Karazan. So how had Karazeel's face got
onto the cover of the game?

Jamie's elbow connected painfully with my ribs.
'*Adam* – wake up! If you're going to be the star of the
show, you might at least pay attention!'

'You OK, son? You look a bit green about the
gills. No need to be nervous – there's nothing to it.
Like I was saying before, all I want you to do is reach
over and turn the computer on. I've already done a
quick test run and made one or two adjustments to the

camera, so we won't have any problems with strobing when we film the screen. While it's doing its stuff just sit quietly. That's when we'll slot in some footage of Mr Quested. Once the booting up's finished, I want you to reach out for the mouse, nice and slow. Don't mind me – pretend I'm not even there. Move the cursor to the Power Quest icon and click. I'll shoot the intro sequence – from what Mr Quested tells us, it's pretty spectacular. Then we'll cut, and do the whole thing over again. All clear?' He gave me an encouraging grin and positioned himself behind the camera; then his cellphone rang again, and he turned away to answer it.

'Adam?' Kenta was looking at me with a worried frown. 'Are you sure you're OK?'

The cameraman was talking rapidly into the phone, sounding hassled. 'Couple more minutes – say ten, fifteen tops – and it's a wrap. Right. *Yes*, dammit, we're moving along as fast as we can!' Scowling, he snapped the cellphone shut and dropped it back in his pocket. 'Sorry, kids, we're running out of time. Busy schedule. Now, Adam: all set?'

'I – I don't know!' I said desperately. I pushed away from the table, my eyes searching for Q. I needed to talk to him . . .

There he was, hovering like a proud parent. He gave me an encouraging beam. 'Just you wait, Adam!' he called over. 'Go on, my boy – turn it on!'

'Yes – come along, son.' The cameraman was starting to sound impatient. 'We haven't got all day!'

I pulled my chair back into position and sat staring at the blank screen. I was conscious of the others grouped round me, bright, artificial looks of excitement on their faces. 'Ready to go?' asked the cameraman.

'I guess,' I croaked.

'Rolling.' Out of the corner of my eye I saw a little red light on the camera blink on. This was it. As if in slow motion, I reached out my hand and pressed the switch on the side of the computer. Stared at the screen as the familiar words flashed across it. Usually, it took forever. But today it seemed only seconds before the last line scrolled up into blackness, and the screen flickered to a marbled blue background with the icons of the six games in the Karazan series arranged in sequence. *Relax, Adam,* I told myself. *What can possibly go wrong? Open the game; get this whole drama over with. Then you can talk to Q – there'll be some kind of logical explanation, you'll see.*

I reached out my right hand and cupped it over the mouse. Moved the mouse a fraction, so the arrow was directly over the Power Quest icon.

Took a deep breath, and clicked.

The screen flicked into darkness, softly diffusing into a momentary glimpse of a road winding away into swirling mist. What could have been a flute played half a bar of eerie, other-worldly music . . . then there was a sudden electronic *ping*, and the screen went totally black.

Nobody moved. We all stared at the blank screen,

fake smiles plastered in place. I guess deep down we were all hoping it was supposed to happen that way – part of Q's stunningly original opening sequence.

Then a tiny dot of light appeared in the very centre of the screen. As we watched, it grew gradually bigger, coming slowly out of the screen towards us. Soon I could see that it wasn't a dot at all, but a line. And then I saw that it wasn't a line, but words, arranged in two sentences, one above the other.

But it was only when it stopped in the centre of the screen, large enough for us all to read, that I saw it wasn't sentences after all. It was random words arranged in two lines, and they didn't make any kind of sense – except for the last two.

stand	*take*	*to*	*King*
we	*you*	*throw*	*Karazeel*

That's when I knew for sure that things had gone terribly wrong.

I looked at Q. His proud beam was still frozen in place; his bow tie had come undone, straggling untidily down the front of his shirt. Somehow the top button had come adrift, and was dangling by a thread.

He took two small, stumbling steps forward. 'This isn't possible,' he croaked.

'Is it . . . part of the game?' quavered Gen.

'*Cut!*' barked the reporter. 'What's going on?' He didn't sound pleased.

'What's happening, Q?' Usherwood hurried up, a

tense frown in place. She took one look at the screen, and the frown deepened. 'Q, I thought you said –'

'This isn't possible,' Q repeated numbly.

'*What* isn't possible? Has something gone wrong?' asked the cameraman.

'It can't have,' said Q.

'Well, it seems that it has,' snapped Usherwood. 'And you *promised* me –'

The cameraman's cellphone went again. He punched a button, growled 'Go *away*!' and snapped it shut. 'Now: what's the story here? What's *that* supposed to mean? I thought you said *stunning visuals*, Mr Quested. Or do they come later?' He glanced at his watch.

'Now, Carl,' crooned Usherwood, 'I'm sure Mr Quested can sort this small hiccup out in a moment. Can't you, Q?' Her voice was sweet as honey, but it didn't fool anyone.

Q hustled forward. 'Yes; yes, of course. If you'll excuse me, Adam . . .' I jumped up so he could have the chair. He stared at the screen for a second in disbelief, shaking his head. His expression was one of complete bewilderment. 'This is quite literally impossible,' he muttered, raising his fingers above the keyboard like a concert pianist preparing to play. His hands were shaking.

There was absolute silence. I expected him to start typing; do a quick fix on whatever was wrong and have us all back on track in moments, like Usherwood had said. But all he did was tap one key with his left index finger: the key on the top left of the keyboard.

Escape.

Nothing happened.

He tapped again, decisively; and again. *Tap . . . tap*. Shook his head. 'I . . . *really*, I don't think you can have any *idea . . .*' He tried one last time. *TAP!*

Nothing changed.

'Well,' he said, his voice trembling slightly, 'I suppose there's only one thing for it. When all else fails . . .' He pressed the Alt key; then Control and Delete, at the same time. I didn't know much about computers, but I did know what that command was for: to restart your computer if it was hopelessly stuck.

But this time, it did nothing at all.

THE IMPOSSIBLE TRUTH

A few minutes later the five of us were still huddled round the computer with Q – but now, we were alone. The TV crew had packed their gear and left, Usherwood hovering behind them making hopeful noises about 'rescheduling at a future date'.

When the door closed behind them, we all heaved a huge sigh of relief.

'Now, Q,' Kenta said gently, 'sit down quietly and try to relax. Explain to us what you think has gone wrong.'

'Will it take long to fix?' asked Rich, ever practical.

'Might it mean postponing the release date, d'you think?' asked Jamie with a worried frown.

Gen didn't say anything – she was staring at the computer screen. As for me – I was watching Q, and the look on his face filled me with dread.

'It's more than that, isn't it, Q?' I said slowly. Some deep instinct told me it all linked in somehow with the shadowy picture of King Karazeel on the cover of the game . . . 'Q,' I began, 'the picture –'

'Hang on a minute, Adam,' said Gen urgently. Her cheeks were flushed and her eyes very bright. 'Those words on the screen, Q – did you write them?'

Q shook his head numbly.

'Well then,' said Rich, 'where the heck did they come from? Things can't just appear out of nowhere!'

'They remind me of something,' murmured Kenta.

'They remind *me* of Karazan,' said Gen grimly, 'and the puzzles that appeared on the parchment in the Temple. Remember how they made no sense at all, and then . . .'

I frowned at the screen. Gen was right – but there was more. 'It's not just about what they mean,' I said. 'Rich is right – if Q didn't write them, how *did* they get here? Where did they come from?'

Even as I said the words, I realised I already knew the answer – to the second question, at least. And as the truth – the impossible, unspeakable truth – slowly crystallised in my mind, Gen spoke quietly in the silent room. '*We* . . . under . . . *stand. You*, under *take. Throw* . . . under *to*? No, that can't be right . . .'

'It's *to*, over *throw*,' said Jamie, looking sick.

'King Karazeel,' whispered Kenta, so softly I could hardly hear her.

My eyes swivelled over to Q, sitting slumped on the chair in front of the computer screen. He didn't look up at me – didn't look at any of us.

'What have I done?' he whispered. 'Oh, children – *what have I done?*'

★

'I still don't understand,' said Jamie. 'OK, so Q's new game – *Power Quest to Karazan* – is about a quest to overthrow an evil king. Sure, there are parallels with the real world of Karazan, but – it's a game, for goodness sake!' His voice rose to an indignant squeak.

'What's real weird is that this message is . . . well . . .' Rich was frowning with concentration, 'that it's from Karazeel. Him, or his sidekick, that creepy Evor. Or both. But how can it be?'

'Karazeel must have found a way of hooking into the link between the computer system at Quested Court and the microcomputer we left in Shakesh,' I said, trying to sound matter-of-fact. Jamie – who'd left the tiny computer behind – blushed scarlet.

'*The VRE interface* . . .' whispered Q. I couldn't bear to look at him.

'So somehow – and this is the bit I really don't understand – Karazeel and Evor have kept tabs on Q while he's been working on his new game . . .' Rich stumbled on. 'And –'

'And now they think it's real – that Q's planning some kind of attack on Karazan,' Gen finished bleakly.

Again, that shadowy face hovered on the fringes of my mind. 'Q,' I asked hesitantly, 'were you aware of anything odd – unusual – when you were working on this game? Different from the others, I mean?'

'Only that it seemed to go so easily – almost writing itself, as I told you before, Adam,' said Q miserably. 'Ideas came into my mind in a . . . a flood of inspiration, like nothing I've ever experienced before. There was such a sense of immediacy . . .'

'The face on the cover of the game,' I asked reluctantly. 'Was that part of it?'

'Yes,' whispered Q. 'It came into my mind as I wrote, as clearly as a face in a dream.'

There was a long, awful silence. Then Rich spoke up, sounding unnaturally hearty. 'So now old Karazeel's got totally the wrong end of the stick. He thinks you're having a go at him, when really it's all just a game. The solution's simple. Tell him.'

At last Q looked up, a flicker of hope in his eyes. 'Tell him?' he repeated. 'But . . . how?'

'Same way he told you,' said Rich with a grin. 'If he can type a message to you, you can send one back. Like e-mail. Let's give it a go!'

Once again, Q raised his fingers over the keyboard. 'I don't see how this can work . . .' he muttered; but then, very slowly, he started to type. While before the keyboard had seemed frozen, now white letters appeared obediently on the screen:

it is only a game

'Full stop,' whispered Jamie. Q typed it in:

.

'What now?' he asked helplessly. None of us knew. We waited.

'Maybe you need to press *Enter* or something,' said Jamie at last, 'to make it –'

Q didn't. Slowly, letter by letter, a reply was appearing on the screen.

> *computer games*
> *mind games*
> *war games*

Then suddenly Q's fingers were flying desperately over the keyboard, rattling off word after word as fast as machine-gun fire:

> *NO!!! It's not REAL don't you see it's all pretend it's got nothing to do with you please don't feel threatened or angry please it's just*

Q's fingers tapped on, but now no new words were appearing on the screen. At last his fingers slowed, and stopped. Again, we waited. Then:

> *the best form of defence is attack*

For a long moment no one said anything. We were all staring at the words on the screen, hardly daring to think what they must mean.

Then the white writing was replaced by a single word:

> *watch*

It hung there for a long moment, suspended in the darkness. Then it dissolved, and in its place appeared a creature, in the very centre of the screen. It was maybe five centimetres tall, three-dimensional and in full colour. At first, only its back view was visible, and for a second I thought it was an armadillo – one of those animals with thick, overlapping armour of gold-coloured scales tapering down to squat, muscular legs and a stumpy tail. But then it rotated, twisting and turning like an astronaut in space, as though someone somewhere was controlling it using a mouse or a joystick . . . and when it was facing us, I saw it was nothing like an armadillo at all.

Its head was covered by small overlapping plates, with tiny, scrunched ears like a hyena. It had the face of a rabid dog, black lips curled back to reveal razor-sharp fangs, eyes burning red as coals with rage and hate. Its hands gripped the hilt of a short, vicious-looking sword with serrations down both edges of the blade. I shuddered to think of the damage they could do.

The creature stared out at us, and for a crazy moment I felt it was somehow really seeing us. Its eyes bored into mine, and it bared its teeth in a silent snarl.

Then, as we watched, the single image suddenly became two: clones of each other, identical in every way, side by side in the blackness. They shrank down tiny in size, so you could hardly make out what they were; then the two became four, the four sixteen, the sixteen a multitude that filled the screen.

'He's copying them,' breathed Jamie. '*Control C*: copy.'

The screen turned black.

'No,' whispered Q. 'He can't do it. There's no way for an adult to pass through the computer, let alone . . . creatures like that. It's impossible – the code that would allow it to happen simply doesn't exist. He's bluffing. He has to be.'

And impossibly, it was as if the computer heard him.

> *the missing code has been written*
> *the creatures of darkness will pass between the worlds*
> *as easily as through an open door*

They were the same words Q had said to us long ago – and somehow that, more than anything, curdled my blood. Staring at the computer screen, I realised that if there had once been a barrier between fantasy and reality, it was there no longer.

The door was open.

Slow and unstoppable, the letters continued to type themselves one by one on the black screen:

soon

THE ONLY PLAN

'If there's even the slightest vulnerability in a system, it's relatively simple for a competent hacker to infiltrate a computer network,' Q told us miserably.

We'd crept out of the computer room as if the walls had ears, shutting the door on that single, menacing word staring out from the black screen. We were in the library with the door closed; Q had lit the fire, even though it was the middle of the day and not particularly cold. We all understood why.

'Yeah,' growled Rich, 'but King Karazeel isn't a compwhatsit hacker. He doesn't even know what a computer is! Karazan's stuck way back in the dark ages as far as all that stuff's concerned, Q – you know that better than anyone!'

'So how . . .' began Jamie. Then suddenly his eyes widened, and his mouth dropped open. 'Oh.'

'Weevil.' It was Gen who said the name that was in all our minds.

'*No!*' said Kenta fiercely. 'He wouldn't! Never! You were wrong about him, Adam! He –'

'Get real, Kenta; he must have. Old Blue-bum's sold us out to Karazeel,' Richard said, shaking his head.

Then slowly, reluctantly, the whole story of Weevil came out, while Q listened in silence.

'But I don't see that it matters!' Richard finished angrily. 'Even if Weevil has changed sides – even if Karazeel is planning to send hordes of computer-generated monsters through the VRE interface – well, it's simple, Q. *Turn the damn thing off!* Unplug it and chuck it in the lake – and that's the end of it!'

But I'd been watching Q's face while we spoke, and seen it settle into a bleak greyness that half-prepared me for his next words. 'From what you've told me, children, your young "friend" is more than competent. The situation is far, far graver than I feared. At first I couldn't understand the extent to which my control over the system had been sabotaged; but now I can. What has happened is this.

'Once the source code of a server has been compromised, it's possible to change a kernel file to give an attacker unauthorised access to operating systems built with the affected source code.

'From there, a program can be created to send improperly formatted remote procedure call messages to a vulnerable machine. Those messages cause a buffer overflow that enables the attacker to place and run their own computer code on the machine, without requiring the owners to open an e-mail attachment, or in fact perform any action at all other than simply turning the computer on.'

'Huh?' said Rich.

'Go on,' said Jamie in an odd little voice.

'The exploit code would open an interface on the vulnerable machine that would enable the remote attacker to issue commands . . . and to take complete control of the system,' went on Q, as tonelessly as if he was reading from a manual.

'I don't get half of that,' said Rich gruffly, 'but I still say: throw the *vulnerable machine* in the drink – now, quick, before something comes crawling out of it!'

But Jamie had gone very pale. 'Don't you all see?' he said. 'It works like a virus – and it's to do with the vulnerable machine, like Richard says.

'But it isn't one vulnerable machine, is it, Q? It's *vulnerable machines* – every single computer belonging to every single kid who's ever bought a copy of a Karazan computer game.'

For a long time, the only sound was the crackle of the fire. Then at last Gen spoke, her voice the merest whisper. 'So some time soon, somewhere in the world, a little kid is going to turn his computer on . . . and it's going to mean the end of everything for all of us.'

Q stared into the fire. Tiger Lily hopped up onto my lap with a soft chirrup, tucked her nose into the crook of her paw, and settled down for a snooze. Automatically, I stroked her silky head, listening to the soothing rumble of her gentle purring.

It would be so easy to imagine everything was OK – the same as it had been an hour ago. But we all knew it wasn't, and never would be again.

A time bomb had started ticking when Jamie left the microcomputer on the guard table in Shakesh . . . or even before that, when Q first had the inspiration for his final game; and now it was about to blow up in our faces.

'And there isn't a single thing we can do about it,' said Rich flatly.

The rumpled plaid rug on the sofa gave a wriggle and a heave, and a dishevelled little head popped out, dandelion hair mussed and face still smudged with sleep. 'Hannah!' cried Q in alarm. 'I had no idea you were here!'

Hannah's eyes were wide awake, and one glance at them told me she'd heard everything. 'Will monsters truly come out of a computer, Q?' she asked solemnly. '*Real* ones – not pretend?'

'No, Chatterbot,' said Q, jumping up and trying to shepherd her to the door. 'Don't you worry your little head about a thing! You run along now and ask Nanny to make you a fairy sandwich for lunch . . .'

I could have told Q he was wasting his time. She wasn't having any of it – not Hannah. 'No!' she said sternly. 'I heard what you were saying, and even though you didn't explain it very well, I understood it all. And I heard what you said too, Richard, about not being able to do anything to stop it happening. Well, you're wrong! There *is* something! It's just like in the dungeon in Shakesh: we have to make Plan B. He hasn't thought of it yet, but he will – won't you, Adam?'

I looked at her. My heart felt like it was made of lead, but I couldn't help smiling. She was still skinny and frail-looking from when she'd been sick, as if a puff of wind would blow her away. But her eyes were bright and fierce, and her starry spikes of white-blonde hair were practically sending out electric sparks of energy and determination. She met my gaze full-on, with a hundred and ten percent confidence and trust.

'Sure I will, Hannah,' I heard myself say. 'You're right: there's always a way. It's just a question of finding it.'

Even as I said the words, I realised I already knew what needed to be done. The knowledge had been there all along, pushed away into the depths of my subconscious. But now I saw clearly there was no other way.

'It's not Plan B, though, Hannah,' I told her. 'This time, there's no Plan A and Plan B. There's only one plan: only one thing we can do. It's simple.' The others were staring at me. I took a deep, deep breath. Once the words were said, there'd be no going back.

'Karazeel was right: the best form of defence is attack. Except it's not him that has to do it: it's us. Just like in Q's computer game, King Karazeel must be overthrown – before it's too late.'

For a long moment, no one said anything. Then Jamie spoke up, putting his finger on the obvious flaw in what I'd said, just like I'd known he would.

'But we can't, Adam! Don't you remember? Hob said so, and Kai. There's only one person who can defeat Karazeel, and it's not us five kids. It's that guy Zephyr, the Lost Prince of the Wind. So you see,' he finished, on a distinct note of relief, 'there's nothing we can do.'

'Yes there is,' I said slowly. 'We can find him.'

A PROMISE TO Q

Talking Q round was harder than I thought. Before, when Hannah's life and safety had been at stake, he'd been quick to see that there was no alternative. But this time, with the whole future of the human race hanging in the balance, he hummed and haa-ed and wrung his hands and wittered away about sending us into danger, until at last Rich ran out of patience. 'Don't you see, Q,' he said bluntly, 'we're in just as much danger if we stay right here. The only difference is that by having a go at finding Prince Zephyr, at least we're in with a sporting chance!'

Q peered unhappily at him through specs more smudged and smeary than I'd ever seen them. 'I know you're right, Richard,' he confessed. 'It's just . . . well . . . I've become so fond of you all, and I feel this is entirely my fault. But I suppose there really is no alternative.

'However, I want you to promise me that if you do manage to find this Zephyr fellow – and for all we know he may be only a legend – you'll leave it to him to sort matters out, and the five of you will come straight home.' Suddenly Q didn't seem like the bumbling, woolly-headed Q we knew: he looked focused and severe, like a normal parent laying down the law. 'I mean this most seriously,' he said sternly. 'I want a solemn promise from each one of you.'

'I promise!' said Jamie.

'So do I,' said Gen. 'After all, Prince Zephyr's the only one who can overthrow Karazeel – once we've found him and told him what's happened, I think we'd probably just be in his way.'

'You're right, Gen,' agreed Kenta. 'I promise, Q.'

Rich looked down, scowling. 'Richard?' said Q quietly.

'But, Q – what if he needs help? What if he needs, like, to be shown the way through the shroud to Shakesh, or something? We –'

'I'm sorry, Richard: you give me your promise, or you don't go.' We could all see Q meant what he said.

'I promise,' muttered Rich with great reluctance.

'Adam?'

'Yeah,' I mumbled. I knew how Rich felt – that finding the Lost Prince would be just the beginning of the adventure. 'I guess I promise too. We'll find Zephyr, and leave the rest to him.'

'You'll come straight home?'

'Yes, we will! We will!' squeaked Hannah, hopping up and down excitedly. 'I promise too, Q – I promise too!'

Q scooped her up in his arms and gave her a kiss. 'You don't need to promise a thing, Chatterbot. You've had all the adventures in Karazan you're ever going to get – you're staying right here to look after me, Tiger Lily and Bluebell!'

'And now, children, I have something for each of you.' Q's face clouded as he moved among us, handing us each a small rectangular object that felt heavy and somehow familiar in the palm of my hand. 'I meant these as a little surprise – a thank-you present, if you like, for everything you've done for Hannah and me. But now . . . well, now at least I'll have the comfort of knowing that no matter what – even if you get separated – each one of you is able to come home again independently of the others.'

I looked down, though I already knew what it was. A microcomputer, virtually identical to the one Jamie had left in the dungeons of Shakesh.

'But I thought –' Jamie began.

Q smiled at him. 'Yes, Jamie: the original was a prototype, the only one in existence at the time. But Nautilus has recently patented the design, and they'll soon be on sale – at a price, mark you. Expensive toys for wealthy executives and their children . . . but no money will ever be able to buy the software I am about to install on yours.' We all knew what he was talking about: the VRE interface that would be our passport back from Karazan.

There was a brief knock on the door and Usher-wood marched in, closely followed by the lumbering figure of Shaw. 'Amazing what a few canapés can do to smooth ruffled feathers,' she remarked smugly. 'I've rescheduled the shoot for the same time next week, Q, and I strongly recommend . . .' She looked from Q to me; from me to each of the others in turn. 'What is it? What's happened?'

The two listened in silence as Q briefly explained. 'So you see, Usherwood,' he finished, 'the children have to go back to Karazan – it's our only hope. I suppose Adam will need your permission, come to think of it . . .'

'An' I don't think yer should give it!' growled Shaw unexpectedly. 'This story about some *Zephyr* bloke sounds like a load o' cobblers ter me – 'oo's ter say he exists at all? An' that computer message – chances are it's just some crazy virus, sent ter put the wind up yer, Q! You're sendin' these kids on a wild goose chase. I say wait an' see wot 'appens – and keep the kids 'ere, where they're safe.'

'Sorry, Shaw – the decision's made,' grinned Rich. 'During the time we're here, Q's in . . . in . . .'

'*In loco parentis*,' supplied Jamie.

'Yeah, that: he's in charge, like my dad said. But thanks for your opinion, anyway!'

I looked across the room at Usherwood. There was an odd look on her face . . . and suddenly I had a sickening premonition that she wasn't going to let me go. 'Ms Usherwood . . . V-V-V-' I gulped, and somehow got it out, in a desperate rush: '*Veronica* – please – they can't go without me!' I knew it was true:

it had to be the five of us, like before. 'Please, please let me go!'

Her lips tightened. She stared at me for a long moment, her expression impossible to read. Then: 'Very well, Adam. You may go with the others – but I hold you to your promise to return at once if and when you accomplish your task.' There was a sudden glimmer of something deep in her eyes. 'And . . . be careful.'

'Yeah – an' bring back ol' Zephyr ter show me if yer find 'im!' grumbled Shaw. He obviously still didn't believe a word of it.

Struggling into my travel-worn jerkin and breeches – tighter than last time I'd worn them, laundered by Nanny, but still holding the faintest hint of the wild, spicy fragrance of Karazan – I found myself thinking back to the other times I'd put them on. The first time, heading off on a quest into the unknown in a desperate attempt to save Hannah's life. The second time: heading back to a world we knew, to rescue her from the clutches of evil King Karazeel.

Now this, the third time . . . and by far the most vital mission of all.

The others knew it too. Even though Q was fussing about like he always had before, warning us to take care of this and remember that, I could see the aloneness I felt reflected in their tense faces.

The game world of Karazan was Q's, but we'd become in some strange way part of the real one. Its destiny was linked with ours. We were just five kids . . . but the weight of the world rested on our shoulders.

At last we were ready. This time, we wouldn't be leaving from the computer room, with its swivel chairs and tidy tables with the peppermints and jugs of water at each place. Instead, we stood in a solemn circle in the library in front of the fire, hands linked. I had my brand-new microcomputer at the ready.

A sense of urgency gnawed at the edges of my mind. We had no time to waste. Richard's hand gripped my arm. I glanced round at the others, then positioned my fingers over the tiny keys.

Alt . . . Control . . . Q.

As I pressed them, a thought flashed into my mind:

If we don't succeed, will there be a world for us to come back to?

A STARTING POINT

I opened my eyes to total darkness. For a heart-stopping moment I thought something had gone horribly wrong – that Karazeel had somehow managed to corrupt the VRE interface so we'd be trapped in nowhere forever.

Beside me I heard a soft whimper, and groped blindly till I felt a cold hand. It gripped mine so tight it hurt. 'Gen?'

'Where are we?' Her voice sounded close to panic.

'In Karazan, of course!' I wondered if Rich felt as sure as he sounded.

'Why it is so dark?' quavered Jamie.

His question was answered by a distant flash of lightning that lit the undersides of the bulging clouds with an eerie purple glow. It was followed a few seconds later by a deep growl of thunder that rolled through the sky like a kettledrum.

'Oh, great,' groaned Jamie. 'The middle of the night, and a thunderstorm on the way! Why isn't time in Karazan the same as at home? Why –'

'Quit grouching, Jamie.' I could hear the grin in

Richard's voice. 'Things could be a lot worse. At least we *are* in Karazan, not stuck in the middle of nowhere like I thought – and by the feel of it, it's summer. We may get a bit wet, but at least we won't freeze!'

From our vantage point at the foot of the cliffs we could see the storm playing out like a gigantic firework display over the sea. There was a steady breeze in my face, carrying with it an electric whiff of cordite mingled with the tang of salt and the fresh scent of rain. 'We're in for a real humdinger, by the feel of it,' I muttered. 'Let's head down into the forest – try to find the clearing we camped in before, and hole up till first light. We could rig a tarpaulin for shelter, and –'

'And put together a plan of action,' interrupted Gen. She was right – we'd left Quested Court with no idea at all of where we were headed, or what to do once we were in Karazan.

'The forest looks awful dark,' quavered Jamie. 'And in the game, there are *things* . . .'

'Yeah,' said Rich bracingly, 'but shrags are scared of light, and we've all got torches. Come on, Jamie – don't be a wimp! Next thing you'll be suggesting we go back to Quested Court and wait by the fire till the storm's over!'

'Well . . .'

'Richard's right – we don't have a choice, Jamie,' said Kenta. 'If we stay here in the open we'll get drenched – and what if the cliff attracts lightning?' As if to demonstrate, a ferocious fork zigzagged from the clouds, striking the distant sea with a sizzle we could almost hear.

'My dad says if there's a storm on the golf course, the last place you should shelter is under a tree,' Jamie muttered; but his words were drowned by an ear-splitting crack of thunder, and drops of rain began to spatter down all round us like water-bombs. There was no more argument – we made a dash for the trees, digging for our torches as we ran.

Moments later we were deep in the forest, hurrying downhill as swiftly and silently as we could. The faint beams of torchlight were nothing like as comforting as Argos' burning brand had been, but it was the best we could do. I kept half an eye open for a glimmer of light from Argos and Ronel's cottage, which I felt sure was over to my left, hidden among the trees . . . but deep down I knew I'd see nothing, and I was right.

The walk seemed to take forever, but at last we were slithering down the steep bank into the familiar grassy clearing. It seemed a different place from the last time we'd been there: the drumming rain had turned the waterfall into a rushing torrent, and the pool had swollen to almost twice the size I remembered. 'We'd better make a bivouac on the higher ground,' Richard shouted above the roar of the rain on the forest canopy way above us. 'Who's to say how far that water might rise – and the last thing we need is for all our gear to be washed away!'

For once no one argued. Rich and I found a long, straight branch, and wedged one end firmly into a cleft in a tree trunk at the edge of the clearing. The others hurried back and forth collecting fallen branches and propping them on either side to make a rough frame the shape of an upside-down V. 'I wish Q had thought to give us proper tents,' panted Jamie.

'This'll do just as well,' said Rich, producing the lightweight plastic tarp from his pack and unfolding it. His curly blond hair was plastered to his head, but nothing could dampen his grin.

Together we spread the cover over our makeshift tent, weighting the edges down with logs. Jamie and the girls didn't need telling: they scampered in and hunkered down as far from the opening as possible, Rich and me right behind them, dragging the packs after us out of the rain.

We huddled together, staring out with wide eyes. The towering trunks of the trees loomed in the blinding after-image of the lightning, and the rain lashed the pool into a hissing cauldron. But we were warm, and the scent of fresh rain and damp, mossy vegetation mingled comfortingly with the more everyday smells of damp clothes and hot feet.

'Anyone for a chocolate bar?' asked Jamie hopefully.

'OK, everybody,' said Gen through a mouthful of chocolate, 'what next? We need to hold a council of war. This rain won't last forever, and once it stops and morning comes, we have to start our search. The only problem we have is . . .'

'We don't have a clue where to look,' finished Richard cheerfully.

'Nor do we have any real idea who we're looking for,' said Kenta. 'It's not as if we had . . . I don't know . . . a photograph, or even a description. How will we recognise Prince Zephyr if we do find him?'

Gloomily, I realised they were right. We'd set off with a hiss and a roar and all the good intentions in the world. The fact was, we were looking for a needle in a haystack . . . a needle we weren't even sure existed.

'Not much point concentrating on what we *don't* know,' I said, licking melted chocolate off my fingers and trying to sound upbeat. 'Let's go over everything we *do* know – everything anyone's ever told us about the legend of Prince Zephyr. Come on, Jamie – you're the one with the almost-photographic memory!'

The dark shape that was Jamie swelled importantly. 'Right: let's start with the basics. His name was – is, hopefully – Zephyr . . . and he's also called the Prince of the Wind.'

'And the True King,' murmured Gen.

'Hob said Prince Zephyr was *born to Queen Zaronel*,' I said slowly. 'I guess that means Queen Zaronel was his mother, and King Zane –'

'– *Good* King Zane –'

'– was his father.'

'But he died,' said Gen. 'What did Kai say? That King Zane lay on his deathbed at that ruined old palace in Arakesh, and when he died, Queen Zaronel's heart *tore asunder*.'

'Yeah – and even old Karazeel went crazy with grief, and ordered the entire place to be smashed up,' said Jamie perkily. 'Though the grief bit doesn't sound very likely to me – from what we saw of him, at any rate.'

'But let's get back to Zephyr – he's the important part!' chipped in Kenta. 'Hob said he was born . . . what was it? . . . *half a hundred spans* ago. A span is a year, so –'

'So that makes him about fifty. More a king than a prince, I'd say,' said Rich.

'I suppose that's the point,' said Gen thoughtfully. 'He's been – what d'you call it? – *in exile*, all this time. And now –'

'Now he's destined to return – *a warrior prince, riding tall and proud on a winged horse*. And on the day he does, he'll be crowned King of Karazan!' finished Jamie with a flourish.

'Way to go, Jamie,' grinned Rich. 'Karazeel will be overthrown, and our world will be safe again . . . and we'll never know how it all happened, because we promised to head home just when the fun was about to begin.'

Jamie gave a gusty sigh. 'To be honest, all that stuff about winged horses sounds a lot like legend to me. We haven't clapped eyes on a single horse in all the time we've been in Karazan – and I'm talking ordinary horses, never mind ones with wings.'

'Even if the legend's true, we can't wait for him to

come riding along in his own sweet time,' Rich pointed out. 'He needs a not-so-gentle nudge, he needs it fast . . .'

'. . . and he needs it from us,' finished Jamie gloomily. There was a long silence, broken only by the steady *drip-drip-drip* of the rain.

'If only we had a tiny clue – just *some* idea of where to start our search!' said Kenta at last. 'Oh, how I wish we'd thought to ask Kai or Hob more about how Zephyr disappeared, and when, and where he might have gone! And if only we'd listened more carefully to what they *did* say!'

'They did say one other thing,' I said slowly, remembering. 'Something maybe we could use as a starting point. We know where he was born: at the Summer Palace in Arakesh. Kai said . . . what was it?' I frowned, Kai's long-ago words hovering on the fringes of my memory like ghosts. As I spoke, they came back into my mind with uncanny clarity, as if Kai himself was standing right beside me. '*Within these walls was born a legend that lives on in tales told by firelight, when voices are low and doors are barred, and dreams stir again in men's hearts.*'

As I said the words, a strange thrill ran through me. For a moment I felt a surge of hope: there was a chance we *would* manage to find Zephyr . . . and when we did, that long-ago baby would have grown into a man, wise and powerful enough to return Karazan to its old glory, and vanquish the threat hanging over our own world.

TO OPEN THE GATE . . .

We woke before sunrise, damp and bedraggled. After a hurried breakfast, we made our way to the edge of the forest where the city of Arakesh lay spread out before us in the misty light of pre-dawn. The gates were closed, the cobbled road leading to them silent and deserted. We skirted the walls, keeping to the shelter of the trees, and soon reached the straggly cluster of bushes that concealed Kai's secret entrance. As we wiggled our way into the tunnel and under the city wall, we heard the distant sound of the gong signalling daybreak and the opening of the gates. With a shudder, I remembered the last time I'd heard that sound, in free fall between two worlds . . . I gave myself a mental shake, and crept on.

One by one the others emerged from the haystack, indistinct shapes in the near-darkness. The stable was still shut up tight, the only light – and the only fresh air – coming from a narrow window set high in the stone wall. The glonks had been in all night, and the stink caught in my throat and made my eyes sting.

We'd tried our best to be quiet, but the bunny ears of the glonks weren't fooled for a moment – and they were expecting breakfast. Our arrival was greeted by a chorus of excited whooffles and burps, farts going off all round us like firecrackers. Rich's dark bulk beside me made a retching sound, and when he spoke his voice was muffled by his cloak, which, like me, he was holding over his nose and mouth. 'Hope the door isn't locked – I won't last more than a couple of seconds in here!'

But luck was on our side, and the heavy door swung open easily to my gentle shove. A wary eye to the gap showed the courtyard of the inn still deserted, though a couple of the windows backing onto the yard were lit with soft golden lamplight. 'Cooking breakfast, I'll bet,' whispered Jamie enviously. 'Bacon and eggs – what wouldn't I give . . .'

'Shhhh! Let's get a move on while the coast's clear!' Heart thumping, I led the way to the arched gate leading out to the lane, lifted the heavy latch and edged it open. It gave a heart-stopping creak, but we were through. Snicking it shut behind us, I followed the others to the mouth of a dark alleyway, where we wiped the smudges of mud from each other's faces as best we could, and picked the bits of straw from our hair.

'Well,' said Rich with a grin, 'we're not exactly clean, but I guess we'll have to do. Let's get moving!'

'Yes, but which way?' asked Jamie unhappily. 'Last

time we had Kai to lead us – I was busy eating my roll and just tagged along behind.'

It was true – none of us had dreamed we'd ever need to find our way back to the palace. Peering out cautiously, I tried to get my bearings. The flaking red and gold sign of the Brewer's Butt was across the narrow lane, the buff-coloured city wall looming behind it. That must be north . . .

Piecing together the few bits and pieces I could dredge up from the depths of my memory, I squatted down and sketched a rough map, using a straw I'd found behind Gen's ear. 'The first time we came, we used the main gate – the one to the east. There were those three streets branching off from the gate like a trident, remember? We took the left-hand fork – the southern one, I guess – leading to the village green where we met Kai.'

'The middle one would have taken us straight to the Temple, I'll bet,' said Jamie.

'Yeah,' chipped in Rich, 'and the right fork would have led through the older part of the city towards Kai's inn . . .'

'And almost directly past the Summer Palace!' squawked Gen triumphantly.

'Come on then, guys – what are we waiting for?' said Rich.

We tramped off down the narrow lane, our hoods pulled well over our faces. The few people we passed hurried about their business, guarded and wary, avoiding our eyes. In our drab, travel-stained clothes we blended in well enough to be almost invisible, I realised with relief – and the Tyrotemp the others had darkened their faces with back at Quested Court completed the camouflage.

Soon the streets began to widen and the higgledy-piggledy houses gave way to larger, more impressive homes. But as we walked on I noticed more and more cracked tiles and crumbling walls; straggly greyish weeds grew up through the cobblestones, and here and there buildings had been partly demolished, jagged stubs of foundation jutting from the ground like rotten teeth.

Glancing up, I saw that tattered grey clouds were gathering, and soon a light drizzle began to fall.

We rounded a corner, and the tall, unbroken wall of the palace stretched ahead. Last time we'd been here, with Kai, all our thoughts had been for Hannah, the Temple and the magical potions, and we'd barely spared it a glance. Now, walking in its shadow, my mind was focused on what – if anything – we'd find inside.

At last we reached the gate. It was a pedestrian entrance set deep into the wall, wide enough for two people to walk through side by side and as tall as a man. The wall continued almost as high again above its arched top. Peering through, we could see a bare courtyard with a broken fountain in the centre, surrounded by covered walkways.

I turned my attention to the gate, and my heart sank. It meant serious business. It was crafted from black wrought iron, heavy and ornate, crusted in places with red rust. Solid hinges attached it to the wall on both sides, and a thick chain was wrapped several times round the curved design in the centre, holding the two halves firmly closed. The chain was covered in cobwebs and obviously hadn't been touched for years. Looking more closely, I saw it wasn't fastened by a bolt or a padlock, as I'd expected; instead, the links were joined by what looked like red sealing wax, imprinted with the familiar twisted crown emblem of King Karazeel.

Beside the gate was a plaque carrying the same symbol, along with the words:

The Royal Seal prohibits entry. Penalty: death.

'Well,' said Jamie, trying to sound disappointed, 'that's that, I guess.'

'That's what?' countered Rich, jiggling the chain and picking at the seal with an experimental fingernail. 'I bet we could chip this wax away in no time flat – it's so old it's crumbling to bits! It was never meant to secure the gate in the way an actual lock would – the threat of being boiled alive by Karazeel does that!'

'But –' quavered Jamie . . . too late. The brittle seal disintegrated between Rich's fingers; crumbs of red wax pattered onto the cobblestones at our feet, and the two halves of the chain fell apart.

'Now you've done it!'

'Looks like it, huh?' grinned Richard. 'That's one less decision to make, anyhow. And if you think about it, Jamie,' he went on comfortingly, 'that threat's

100

pretty empty as far as we're concerned. If Karazeel finds out we're back in Karazan we're dead meat, seal or no seal.'

He unwound the chain, and it slid to the ground with a harsh metallic clatter that made us all check anxiously over our shoulders. But there was no one in sight, for the moment at least.

'Hurry – let's get inside before someone comes!' hissed Gen, her eyes wide with fright.

Rich grasped the two halves of the gate and gave a firm shove. They didn't budge. Frowning, he pulled the other way. They didn't move. We could all clearly see the wafer-thin, unbroken line of light between the two halves; there was nothing holding them together, except . . .

'You don't think they could be . . . well . . . magic in some way, do you?' whispered Gen, echoing my thoughts. 'This is Karazan, don't forget. Maybe the chain and seal were Karazeel's way of saying *Keep out, or else*, but the gates are actually *locked* by . . . I don't know . . . a spell, or something.'

After a quick glance up and down the deserted street, we all stepped back and had another good look at the gate. Staring at it – and really seeing it for the first time – I knew in my heart that Gen's suggestion was right. What I'd originally dismissed as decorative swirls seemed to take on a deeper, more mysterious significance, and I could tell by Jamie's sigh and the others' gloomy silence that they felt the same.

'Look – across the top, engraved in the metal,' said Kenta. 'It's so rusted and weatherworn you can hardly read it, but I think it says: *To open the gate . . .*'

'Yeah – but to open the gate, what?' growled Rich. Now that there was a puzzle rather than a chain to unravel, I knew he felt the way I did: useless and stupid.

'Maybe it carried on somewhere else – on the horizontal crosspiece, say – and Karazeel had it erased so no one could get in,' suggested Jamie.

'Can't see any sign of anything,' said Rich, peering at the rough, pitted surface dubiously.

'The design is odd, isn't it?' said Gen thoughtfully. 'That curved hieroglyph thing – those funny angular specs – repeated inside the circles. You don't suppose the rest of the clue – the bit that tells you *how* to open the gate – is somehow in the actual design of the gate?'

'I don't see how,' grumbled Rich. 'Though it would be typical Karazan.'

'They're not glasses,' said Kenta suddenly. 'It's the number five, mirrored.'

'Huh?'

'Kenta's right.' Jamie pointed with a chubby finger. 'A 5, see? And here again, turned back-to-front: 5.'

'Five . . .' repeated Gen softly. We looked round at one another, the same thought in all our minds. *Five* . . . suddenly I felt certain we were on the right track.

'Are the circles numbers too, then, d'you think?' asked Jamie. 'Noughts, perhaps? Zeros?'

TO OPEN THE GATE

'To open the gate,' Gen was murmuring, 'to open the gate . . . mirror five? Turn five?'

I kept quiet, glad I hadn't said what I was thinking. I'd got it wrong as usual, just like at school. Instead of seeing a five and a zero, I'd seen the shapes as eights, side by side, in a kind of square . . . and lying on their sides, one on top of the other. *Zero for you, Adam Equinox*, I thought with a wry grin. *Some things never change – even in Karazan.* Listening to the others with half an ear, I ran my fingers absently over the cold metal. First one circle, anti-clockwise; then the one beside it, clockwise . . . then back again, round and round in figures-of-eight, my mind drifting . . .

Then Gen was clutching my hand, squeezing so hard my fingers cracked. 'That's it, Adam! You've got it! They're not zeros: they're eights! The number 8!'

'They could be, I suppose,' said Kenta dubiously, 'though it still doesn't make any sense.'

'It does! It completes the rhyme,' jabbered Gen, practically dancing with frustration. 'That's how I know it must be right! To open the gate, *turn 5 . . . into 8!*'

'And how the heck do we do that?' growled Rich. 'Turn the *five* of us into *eight*, d'you think? Clone ourselves, like old Karazeel and his monsters? Or grab three strangers off the street and ask if they'd mind risking being strung up . . .' He saw the hurt look on Gen's face and wound down, looking sheepish.

'Could the missing three be Kai and Hob . . . and Bl– Weevil, maybe?' said Kenta hesitantly. 'Except . . .'

'Except Hob doesn't ever want to see us again, Kai's in Shakesh, and old Blue-bum's frolicking in the treetops who knows where,' finished Rich. 'And we need the gate open now, not in six months' time.'

The grim reminder of how little time we had silenced us all.

An image of Hannah's face flashed into my mind, eyes round as saucers: *Will monsters truly come out of a computer? Real ones – not pretend?* I remembered my own words to her: *There's always a way. It's just a question of finding it.* It was the truth – it had to be. I believed it with all my heart; but if I was afraid of making a few mistakes along the way . . .

'We know it's to do with five,' I said slowly, staring at the gate. 'Five *somethings* . . . There are five bars.' I felt myself turn bright red, but soldiered on. 'At the bottom . . .'

'Yeah!' yipped Jamie. 'Five bars! So all we have to do is turn the five bars into eight . . .'

There was a long silence.

'Maybe we're on completely the wrong track,' said Gen at last. 'Or maybe there's another gate somewhere . . .'

'We could try climbing over . . .' But following Rich's gaze to the top, I knew it wasn't an option. The gate was too deeply recessed, and the wall way too high.

'Turn five into eight,' Jamie was muttering, like a dog with a bone.

'There's no way, Jamie,' said Richard bluntly. 'You

can't turn five bars into eight. It's impossible. We've gone wrong somewhere.'

Jamie ignored him, staring intently at the bars with folded arms and narrowed eyes, as if he was willing them to rearrange themselves into the number we needed. Then all of a sudden his eyes popped wide open and he punched the air. '*It's Roman numerals!*'

'He's finally cracked,' said Rich, shaking his head. 'Poor old Jamie . . . all that maths extension's blown his brain.'

'You're right, Richard – it *is* all thanks to maths extension!' Jamie's eyes were shining. 'What's the number 8 in Roman numerals?' He looked from face to face expectantly. So did Rich, and so did I. The answer wasn't coming from either of us, that was for sure.

It was Kenta who said hesitantly, 'Five is V . . . so would it be . . . V . . . III?'

Every eye swivelled from Jamie's flushed face to the gate. Then Jamie stepped forward, crouched down, and grasped the two left-hand bars firmly in both hands. There was a slight grating sound, and then the bases of the bars slid smoothly together. They touched with a faint metallic click . . . and the gate vanished as if it had never existed.

THE SUMMER PALACE

'We're in!' said Rich, rubbing his hands. 'Come on, guys – what are you waiting for?'

'I just hope the gate comes back once we're through,' said Gen bleakly. 'Because if it doesn't . . .'

'. . . the first person who walks past is going to know there's someone inside – and then what?' finished Kenta, looking sick.

'Let's worry about that if it happens. Come on!'

We hustled through the gate into the courtyard, then turned and looked hopefully at the arched gap. 'There's probably a special way of closing it again . . .' said Jamie.

'Well, we don't have time to mess around trying to figure it out! Someone could come by at any moment . . . with any luck they'll think it's Karazeel's heavies doing a spring clean or something. Let's head inside, have a quick scout around and see what we can find – and then get the heck out of here!'

We hurried through the nearest archway into the gloom of the interior. There was a feel of damp air long undisturbed, of pale, watery light and crouching shadows. I saw majestic columns fallen into ruin, cracked flagstones, crumbling masonry. The past drifted in the air like a ghost, brushing my skin with invisible fingers.

'The whole place seems to have been smashed up, like Kai said,' whispered Jamie. 'If there were ever any clues, they would have been wrecked or taken years ago.'

'Still, we need to look. Perhaps we should split up to explore,' suggested Kenta. 'This place is huge – it'll take us hours to search it all.'

'Especially seeing we don't know what we're looking for,' said Gen. 'But what if one of us gets lost? I think we ought to stay together.'

'Let's explore in pairs,' Jamie suggested. 'You can come with me, Gen. I've got a really good sense of direction, plus I've done orienteering in Scouts.'

'I'll go with you, Kenta,' offered Rich. 'Though that leaves Adam . . .'

'I'll be fine,' I said quickly. Truth was, the thought of wandering through the deserted rooms on my own had an odd attraction.

There were waterproof digital watches in one of the inner compartments of our packs. We synchronised them, agreeing to meet back at the gate in an hour.

The others headed off purposefully, peering into shadowy corners, calling and exclaiming, their voices echoing back to me long after they had disappeared. I stood quietly, waiting for the silence to settle again.

At last I walked slowly in the opposite direction, deep into the labyrinth of rooms, my feet making almost no sound on the stone floors.

Kai had said the Summer Palace had once been beautiful, filled with music and laughter. Now all that remained was an empty shell. I reached a huge rectangular hall I imagined might once have been a throne room; with its soaring ceiling and arched windows it reminded me of a church, or a cathedral. Gazing up, I could make out remnants of stained glass in one of the windows, and a bird's nest tucked into the corner of the sill.

I moved out into what had once been a garden, bare skeletons of trees grouped beside cracked fountains, tangled grass grown rank and wild. On the far side was a deep pool, fragments of peacock-blue, turquoise and emerald-green mosaic still clinging to its fissured sides. A piece of mosaic the shape of a teardrop, sea-green inlaid with shimmering gold glitter, caught my eye, almost hidden in the grass; automatically, I picked it up and slipped it into my pocket.

Once that pool would have held sparkling water; now it was empty apart from a greenish puddle. Had Prince Zephyr swum here when he was a boy? Had he taken his first steps on the level lawn, his laughter mingling with the music of the fountains? In the bare, bleak place the Summer Palace had become, it was hard to imagine.

A tall, turreted building adjoined the pool. It was set slightly apart from the main palace, almost as if it was a private dwelling. I stepped inside, staring round me. Doorways led off to left and right; ahead, a stone staircase curved out of sight. Curious, treading warily, I followed it upwards.

The steps were worn to a satiny smoothness, lit by narrow windows set into the wall. The stairway opened onto a landing where a porcelain urn lay smashed on its side, the plinth it once stood on leaning drunkenly against the wall. A rug that would once have been deep wine-red lay crumpled beside it, faded by time to a dull rose.

I stepped quietly through double doors of honey-coloured wood into another, larger room. It must be above the city wall, I realised: arched casements opened out onto light and space and a distant view of the sea. On one windowsill a small brown bird trilled a few bars of song, then spread its wings and was gone. The early morning cloud had burned off; sunlight streamed through the window, gilding the wood panelling and warming the faded scarlet silk that lined the far wall.

Suddenly I realised where I must be. *Red was the colour of royalty* – I had stumbled on the private chambers of King Zane and Queen Zaronel. For the first time, I felt like an intruder.

The room I was in was a bedchamber – and unlike the rest of the palace, relics of furniture remained. What had once been rich tapestries, blowing in ragged tatters in the light breeze drifting through the window. An empty wardrobe, one door hanging crazily from a twisted hinge. A four-poster bed with an interlocking crown embroidered in gold and silver on its scarlet canopy, the uprights scarred by vicious hack-marks. What I guessed might have been bedclothes lay tumbled in one corner, beside a huge, carved chest that had been upended and smashed almost to splinters. Whatever it had once held was long gone.

Even now, after so many years, a residue of rage and violence hung in the air. I could feel it, like the vibration left by a scream after the sound has died away. I closed my eyes, trying to tune in to the echoes of the past . . .

Karazeel had ordered this to be done. *Crazed with grief after King Zane's death* – or so Kai said. But in my mind I could see the twist in Kai's mouth, hear his bitter, ironic tone. Now I realised his words had been a mockery of the truth: a truth that stabbed through me with the certainty of a sword.

Karazeel had been searching for something.

But what? And had he found it . . . or was it still here, hidden in the wreckage that remained?

THE CHAMBER OF THE KING

I moved slowly into the centre of the room. To one side was a small vestibule with an arched doorway; through it I could see a marble shelf holding a shallow bowl and matching jug, both smashed to pieces. Near the window an ornate desk lay overturned, its drawers scattered nearby. There was no sign of whatever they had once held.

In the far corner, a glint of metal caught the sun. I hurried over and picked them up: two heavy gold coins, with a crowned head on one side and a coiled serpent on the other. I stared down at the face of King Zane. It was in profile, impassive, stern and regal. Strong features; a wide, clear brow. Eyes that gazed unflinchingly to the future – a future he was never to see.

I slipped the coins into my pocket and moved on.

As I passed the tapestry beside the bed, I paused to look at it more closely. The brass rod that supported it had been wrenched from the panelling and hung crookedly, the tapestry bunched at one end. It was faded by the sun and mildewed in one corner where

112

the rain blew in off the sea. I could make out some kind of hunting scene – what looked like a boar, with a group of men on horseback in pursuit. *So there had been horses once . . .*

I smoothed it out to have a closer look . . . and the support gave way completely, dumping a double armful of heavy, musty-smelling cloth on top of me. Instinctively I clutched it to me, but the rod slid out of its sleeve and fell to the floor with a ringing clatter. Wincing, I lowered the whole lot to the ground; then straightened and glanced at the wall where it had hung, wondering what the chances were of replacing it. Not that it would matter if I left it where it was . . .

And then I noticed something odd.

The wall beside the bed was made of wood: rectangular panels with bevelled edges like expensive picture frames. The wood was beautiful: rich and perfect, the natural grain of the wood patterning the smooth surface like a breeze on still water. It must have been faded by the sun over the years, because the place where the tapestry had hung was darker than the rest . . . and in the corner of one of the panels there was a knothole. Normally, you wouldn't have looked at it twice. But not in that room – the Chamber of the King – and on that flawless panelling.

Frowning, I looked closer, running my finger over it.

It was at eye level, and completely circular. The wood at its centre was darker than the rest, with a deep indent surrounding it. It looked almost like a button or a switch, concealed in the panelling.

My pulse quickening, I reached out one finger, placed it in the exact centre of the circle, and pressed. Nothing happened. But this was Karazan, and every instinct told me I was right: it was there for a reason. It had to be. Was it possible that the middle part turned, like a key? I tried to get a grip on it, but the gap between the knob and the surrounding wood was too narrow. I put my thumb firmly on the centre and twisted, but it turned uselessly on the smooth surface. I needed something that would grip like a spanner, something circular, that would fit into the groove . . .

I shoved my hands into my pockets, scowling with frustration – and my fingers felt the golden coins. *Maybe – just maybe* . . . I held a coin up to the knothole, but it was way too big. Also, it was flat, and I needed something with a rim. But it had started me thinking: what else might do? A screw-on lid! Squatting on the floor, I dug through my backpack and unearthed my drink bottle. One glance showed me it would be pretty close. Quickly I unscrewed it and fitted it to the knothole. For a tantalising second the edge caught and my heart gave a skip of hope . . . but then it slid off. Also too big, by a hair's-breadth.

But I was convinced I was on the right track. I scanned the room for something – anything – that might fit. As it always did when I was thinking hard, my hand moved to the rough outline of the ring under my shirt . . . and still, it was a long moment before the thought consciously registered in my mind. My ring! I was so used to wearing it that I barely thought about it – it was as much part of me as my hands and feet. But it was the right shape, and about the right size . . .

I felt for the knot in the bootlace and tugged it round so I could untie it. It took forever – it had pulled tight, and my fingers were clumsy with excitement. But at last it was undone, and I slid the ring off. It lay in my palm, its silver sheen soft in the dusty sunlight. Out of long habit I ran my fingers over its familiar contours, smooth at the back, heavier and deeply ridged at the front; then, without thinking, I slid it on. All my life it had been way too big for me, but it had been a long time since I'd last worn it, and now it fitted almost perfectly.

I slipped it off and held it up to the wall. For a moment I thought it was going to be too big, and the metal too wide to fit the narrow groove. But then I tried again, tilting it slightly to adjust the angle . . . and it slotted in like it was made to measure, with just enough protruding for me to grip between my finger and thumb. I twisted gently clockwise. Nothing. The other way . . . the ring turned as smoothly as a key in a lock, and I felt the panelling move beneath my hand.

And at the same moment, I heard the soft scuff of a footstep on the stairs.

NO PLACE TO HIDE

The ring dropped back into my hand as I spun to face the door, staring wildly round for a place to hide, my mind racing. *They'd seen the open gate . . . they were hunting us down, and the clatter of the falling rod had led them here, to the turret room. I was trapped.*

In three long strides I was over at the vestibule, shoving the ring and bootlace into my pocket. It was a tiny alcove – barely more than a metre square – but I flattened myself into the corner behind the archway, praying the narrow architrave would shield me from view. If they stopped at the door, there was a chance I'd be safe . . . but if they came into the room, I'd be seen for sure.

Every sense sharpened by the adrenaline pumping through me, I could hear them clearly over the hollow thudding of my own heart: several sets of soft footfalls sneaking stealthily up the staircase.

There was the faintest creak as the door opened, and the ragged, panting breaths of hunters on the scent. Then came two soft sniffs, as if something was tasting the air . . . then a longer one, a phlegmy snuffle that turned my blood to ice. *The Faceless wouldn't need eyes to find me, no matter how well I was hidden . . .*

Then the silence was broken by a whisper: a voice I recognised, that turned my knees to jelly with relief. 'Jamie, do you need a tissue?'

'Sorry –' an apologetic mumble – 'it's the dust . . .'

The sound of someone blowing their nose – not Jamie's usual honking blast, but a much more subdued version – was followed by a furious '*Shhhh!*' from Rich.

Then came Gen's voice, a desperate undertone on the edge of tears. 'He isn't here! I could have sworn I heard a noise . . . what are we going to *do*?'

I stepped out from my hiding place with a sheepish grin. 'Hi, guys,' I began, realising that for some reason, like them, I was whispering. 'I thought –'

I was interrupted by a thunderous sneeze. It was the kind of sneeze that sneaks up on you from behind and practically takes the top of your head off, flattening everything in its path and rupturing the eardrums of people nearby with a sonic blast of sound. If a sneeze like that happens at school, you know right off it'll be a good five minutes before everyone picks themselves up off the floor and stops laughing.

But no one was laughing now. Jamie clapped his hand over his mouth as if he was trying to somehow stuff the sneeze back in. Gen turned white as a sheet.

And from outside came hoarse shouts, the hiss of steel blades being drawn from scabbards, and the thud of booted feet approaching at a run.

'We saw them coming – guards, and one of *them* . . .' Gen's face crumpled. 'We tried to find you –'

We had seconds at best.

There was no time to think; no time to do anything except act – fast. I hadn't given the slight shift of the panelling under my hand another thought – but now I knew it was our only hope. 'Quick,' I breathed, 'this way!'

At the slightest pressure from my hand, a section of wall the size of a low door moved inwards into blackness, opening as smoothly and silently as if on oiled hinges. The others didn't need telling: without a word they ducked inside and disappeared. I followed them, easing the door closed again behind us. With a sliver of light still visible I hesitated, the memory of that long-ago dream surfacing in a suffocating rush . . . what if we couldn't open it again?

Then I felt the chill presence of the Faceless in the room beyond – not nightmare, but reality. I pushed the door closed and we huddled in the blackness, waiting.

The sounds on the far side of the door were muffled and indistinct. I could feel the vibrations of heavy footsteps, hear broken fragments of words and the grinding squeal of furniture being dragged out of place and crashing to the floor. There was no doubt – they knew we were here.

We cowered in the pitch dark, hardly daring to breathe. *Please*, I thought numbly; *please don't let them see it* . . .

I felt a coldness seep through the door. In my mind's eye I saw a hooded head, and smelled the sickening stench of decay. Behind me, I heard the tiniest catch of a sob. I reached back and felt for Gen's hand, squeezing it in warning. A sound reached us faintly through the wood: a soft, exploratory scrabbling.

Then a man's voice spoke from what seemed right beside me, harsh and commanding. 'Behind the wall – a chamber? A keyhole . . . why was this not found before? You: fetch axes – now! And give me your sword!'

A second's pause, and then a blow like a sledgehammer smashed into the wood beside my head with a force that sent me reeling backwards, hands to my face. But the door was heavy and solid; it hadn't broken through – yet.

I groped in the darkness for the others, shepherding them backwards, as far from the door as I could. Blindly, drawing them after me, I stumbled back . . . back . . . back into the utter blackness, expecting at any moment to come up against the solid resistance of a wall. And gradually, with each shuffling step, it dawned on me: *It wasn't a room, it was a passage* . . .

Rich's voice huffed in my ear: 'You go on ahead, Adam; I'll make sure no one's left behind. *Hurry!*'

As quickly as I dared, testing the ground ahead of me, feeling my way along the cold stone walls with my

hands, I led the others back into the tunnel. One step
. . . two . . . three . . . then, on the left, the wall disappeared under my groping hand. I stumbled to a
halt, disoriented. Was it a bend in the tunnel? Or . . .

The rhythmic crashes from behind us had changed.
They were heavier now: axe-blows, massive and crip-
pling, sending shock waves through the tunnel after
us. I could barely hear Jamie's trembling whisper:
'Adam? Shall I get out my torch?' or Gen, close to
panic: '*No* – they might see the light!'

I fumbled at the wall like a blind man, trying to
build up a picture in my mind. No – it wasn't a bend,
or a tunnel. It was a recess in the wall . . . a niche, as
deep as my forearm, with an arched top and a flat base
like a shelf . . . 'Come on, Adam – hurry *up*!' There
was another shuddering crash from behind us.

'*Wait* . . .' My fingers had found something on the
shelf . . . some *things* . . .

A dense, flat object . . . a floppy block that released
a familiar, dusky scent when I picked it up. And
something else: a smooth, cool cylinder . . . I slipped
them both into my pocket, then turned away, trailing
my fingers over the bare surface . . . They brushed
against something small and soft as a cobweb. I closed
my fingers, feeling – or imagining – something
between them . . . and shoved it deep into my pocket
with the rest.

'*Hurry!*'

Rich was right – there was no time to waste. I
headed into the blackness at a shuffling run – and then

120

without warning the ground disappeared under my feet and I was falling, tumbling over and over, invisible walls cracking my elbows and knees, stone steps connecting with my kidneys like steel-toed boots. At last the floor met the back of my head with a dizzying *smack* and I lay dazed, my legs in a tangle, a galaxy of blue stars spinning in the blackness.

From somewhere way above, punctuated by the rhythmic double *kerTHWACK-kerTHUNK* of the axe-blows, a trembling thread of a whisper wound its way down to me: '*Adam . . . Adam . . . are you OK?*'

I struggled to my hands and knees, trying to figure out which way was up and whether my legs and arms were still attached. I'd curled into a ball when I fell, instinctively wrapping my arms round my head for protection, so my back had taken the brunt of the impact when I'd somersaulted down the steps; as far as I could tell nothing was broken. 'I . . . I'm fine – I think,' I croaked, finding the wall with an unsteady hand and levering myself to my feet. Quickly I checked my pockets: my ring was still there; so were the rectangular package and the cylinder, miraculously intact. 'It's a stairway – a steep one,' I called softly. 'Come down carefully!'

Turning, I tried to get my bearings again. The stairway was behind me, and once again there were solid walls on either side. I moved forward, more cautiously this time, feeling my way . . . but then – impossibly – my searching hands found stone. It couldn't be. The stairway wouldn't lead nowhere!

I groped sideways, then upwards, my fingers – suddenly slick and greasy with sweat – probing desperately for a passage, a gap, an opening just large enough for us to squeeze through . . .

There was nothing. We were caught like rats in a trap.

SOMETHING OR NOTHING

From behind us came a splintering smash and a hoarse, triumphant yell. The faintest suggestion of grey light seeped into the passage, carried on a breath of fetid air.

They had broken through.

'It's a dead end,' I said flatly, turning to face the others. 'We can't go on.'

Kenta's voice came fiercely out of the darkness. '*No!* There was a way to get in – there *must* be a way to get out! We can't give up! We *won't!*'

A way to get in . . . at last my mind stopped running in circles and logic took over. Kenta was right – I was certain of it. We could get out – the same way we got in.

There was no time to explain. The shouts and crashes were growing louder and more urgent. I could almost see the gaping hole widening with every blow . . .

I forced myself to be calm. Turned back to the wall, closed my eyes and concentrated, exploring the granular surface of the rock with my fingertips like a blind person reading Braille. *It would be at eye level, like before* . . . and then I felt it. My finger traced it, light as a feather: the outline of a circle, indented in the stone. My hands were shaking as I fumbled for my ring.

Once, twice the ring slipped out of the groove; then it caught and held. I twisted; felt it turn. Pushed it back into my pocket, then set my shoulder to the wall and heaved, my feet slipping on the smooth floor. The rock grated, then gave, a massive shoulder-high section of stone inching reluctantly outward. I heard Rich's grunt as he threw his weight beside mine . . . one last catch, and white light exploded in my face as the huge door swung open, as slow and heavy as the steel door of a vault.

First Gen, then Jamie squeezed through the gap; Kenta was next, then Rich, helped along by a shove from me. I ducked after him, then spun and threw myself against the rock to close it again. Rich was beside me, and Jamie, his face purple with effort . . . the girls were heaving from behind. But the door wouldn't budge.

Through the crack we heard the guards break through the last defences of the inner door: a roar of triumph rolled down the tunnel like a wave of dark water, booted feet echoing like drums as they charged towards us.

I gathered all my strength into one last, desperate effort, my chest bursting, every muscle on fire . . . my eyes were fixed on the ground, and that's how I saw it.

A flint – a small, wedge-shaped stone – jammed under the base of the door. One of us must have kicked it there in our rush to get out. '*Wait!*' I panted; grasped the heavy doorjamb with both hands and flung my weight backwards, heaving with all my might. The door moved back – the merest touch, but enough. I bent, snatched up the stone and flung myself against the door one last time, the others with me . . . and now there was no resistance. As if on invisible hinges, the huge slab of stone slid silently back into place.

We stood, sweaty and panting, staring at the bare wall. It was as if the door had never been there at all. And on the other side – who knew? There wasn't the faintest whisper of sound; not the slightest vibration.

We were outside the city wall, to the north. A short distance away was the edge of the forest. Birds fluttered and twittered in the trees; cotton-wool clouds floated above us in a blue sky.

Rich gave us a slightly shaky grin. 'Now *run!*' he said; and we ran.

Into the shelter of the trees, deeper and deeper into the forest we ran. Leaping over fallen tree trunks, ducking under branches, slithering down banks and scrambling up the other side, pushing through dense undergrowth, splashing for what seemed like hours along a shallow creek to hide our scent, our feet slipping and sliding on the pebbled river bed.

Even knee-deep in water Rich barely slowed his pace, glancing over his shoulder every now and then to check we were managing to keep up. I stayed at the back of the group, ready to offer help or encouragement if anyone needed it – Jamie especially. But he slogged on through the icy water, puffing like a steam train, pop-eyed with determination. Sensing me watching him he turned and gave me a thumbs-up, then almost lost his footing and frantically windmilled his arms to keep his balance, practically taking my head off. Closer to the bank the girls struggled on grimly, holding hands to keep their balance, murmuring the occasional word to each other for comfort.

At long last we left the river behind, clambering up the mossy, overgrown bank and up through lacy ferns and leafy saplings that gave off a pungent, peppery scent when we brushed past. The ground rose steadily for a while and then levelled out, the forest stretching endlessly away ahead of us.

Finally Rich slowed to a walk, then stopped and waited for us, wiping his sweaty face on his sleeve. Jamie came up level with him and collapsed like a popped balloon; my legs turned to putty and I flopped down next to him, digging in my pack for water.

We were in deep shade. There was no way of telling what time it was, and though occasional golden glimmers of sunlight caught the edges of leaves high overhead, it was impossible to guess its direction. But one thing was for sure: it would be hard for anyone, even the Faceless, to follow our trail.

'Before any of you ask,' said Rich, taking a long pull at his canteen, 'I don't have a clue where we are.

We're totally lost – and I don't know about the rest of you, but I'm in no hurry to be found again.'

'Well,' said Gen ruefully, pushing her tangle of hair back from her flushed face, 'so much for finding anything useful in the Summer Palace.'

Believe it or not, it was only then that I remembered. 'Hang on – I did find something.' I heaved myself to my feet and dug in my pocket. 'In the tunnel, when I stopped: there was a kind of shelf . . .'

I brought out my hand and opened it slowly. There in the palm lay a cylinder of gleaming bluish-grey metal. It was about as thick as my thumb and twice as long, rounded at both ends. I turned it, peering at it in the leafy gloom, trying to figure out what the heck it could be. It didn't seem heavy enough to be solid . . . though in Karazan, who knew? Shrugging, I passed it on to Gen.

Another dig, and out came the flat package – and here at least there was no doubt what it was. A book. A pocket-sized book that reminded me with a pang of my *Bible*; but while that had been brown, this was a rich crimson – almost maroon – embossed with faded letters in gold.

I held it up to the light, and read slowly aloud:

Book of Days

'Open it!' ordered Jamie excitedly. 'It must be a clue!'

My pulse quickening, I thumbed open the cover. The parchment inside was far more delicate than any we'd seen before, cream-coloured – I squinted at it in the gloom – with a faintly marbled finish. I raised it to my face and breathed in. Underlying the warm animal fragrance of leather I thought I could detect a hint of a different, more subtle perfume, as if the paper itself had been scented once, long ago . . .

'Come on, Adam – read it, don't eat it!' said Rich impatiently.

I turned over the first page. It was blank. So was the next, and the next. I flipped to the end and riffled through the pages from back to front, scanning them for any sign of writing.

There was nothing. The book was completely empty. I looked up and saw the others staring at me with hopeful, expectant faces. 'Sorry, guys,' I said flatly. 'It's a dud. Whatever a *Book of Days* is, this one hasn't been written in. It isn't going to tell us a thing.'

'Hang on, let me see . . .' Jamie reached out a grubby hand and I passed it over. He was welcome to look, but I knew he'd see exactly what I had: nothing.

Rich spoke up, his voice hollow. 'Was that all?'

'Yeah, I'm afraid so. Though I did find these in the bedroom . . .' My fingers felt the chink of metal. I fished out the two coins and the piece of mosaic, along with the rest of the crud you find at the bottom of pockets, and dropped the whole lot in the palm of my hand. 'The coins could come in useful, I guess,' I said hopefully, passing them round for the others to see. 'But other than that, it's just bits and pieces I've picked up along the way – and fluff and stuff.'

The memory of that whisper of feeling on my finger-tips in the dark niggled at the back of my mind. *Had* it been something – or nothing? Or had I dropped it – whatever it was? I gave the sorry little pile a poke with my finger, scowling at it doubtfully. There was the wedge-shaped stone that had stopped the stone door from closing; crumbs, and sand, and tiny balls of cotton; a long, tapered filament of something that looked like stiff nylon . . . I picked it up, puzzled, then grinned.

A Tiger Lily whisker! What else? Among the bits was a tiny feather, palest grey shading to silver, with three faint white bands at the tip like miniature new moons, or a three-tiered rainbow. I held it up, feeling like a prize idiot. 'I thought there was something else . . . this might have been it, I guess . . .'

'But that's just a feather!' said Rich, unimpressed.

'I dunno, Richard.' Jamie clambered to his feet and came over to look. 'It could be magical. There must be a reason for it being there, after all.'

Rich rolled his eyes. 'Get real, Jamie! Just being in the secret passage doesn't automatically make it some kind of holy relic. That shelf would have got covered in all sorts of rubbish over the years – bird bones and bat shit and stuff like that. Lucky you didn't pick up a handful of that too, Adam! Well done finding the book and the coins and the . . . cylinder-thing, though.' I knew he was thinking – but tactfully not saying – *for all the good they might ever be.*

'I'm afraid I agree with Richard for once,' said Gen

apologetically. 'Sometimes a feather's just a feather, even in Karazan.'

I stowed the book and the cylinder safely away in my backpack, and was on the point of tipping the junk collection onto the ground when something stopped me. Turning away so the others wouldn't tease me, I slipped the whole lot back into the depths of my pocket – and promptly forgot all about it.

'And now,' said Jamie, sounding determinedly cheerful, 'who's for a handful of scroggin and a look at the map?'

A LITTLE BIT OF MAGIC

I watched Kenta haul out the bulging bag of scroggin and pass it round. Hannah had helped Nanny make it for us back at Quested Court. 'You take it on long walks and adventures,' she'd told me solemnly. 'It's called scroggin because those are the first letters of all the ingredients: sultanas, chocolate, raisins, orange peel – the candied kind, ginger (though you leave that out 'cos it's yucky), glucose, imagination, and nuts. Glucose is another word for barley sugars.'

'Imagination?' I asked her, pretending to be puzzled. 'How can you put *imagination* in a recipe? You can't eat it, can you?'

'Yes you can – Q says so! He says it's the *food of the soul*: a little bit of this and a little bit of that, spiced up with magic. And when I make scroggin with Nanny, that means . . .'

Hundreds and thousands. Now, deep in a forest somewhere in Karazan, there they were: a rainbow-coloured drift in the bottom corner of the bag. Smiling, I helped myself to a double handful of the

131

scroggin, making sure I got plenty of chocolate and not too many raisins. I was about to pop the first piece of chocolate into my mouth when I stopped and had a closer look at it. There, indented in the shiny brown surface, was a small, perfect fingerprint, lined with tiny multicoloured balls.

'It shouldn't be too hard to figure out where we are – more or less, at any rate,' Jamie was saying with his mouth full, holding out one hand to Kenta for the map.

It had been Jamie who'd found it – or more accurately pinched it, though admittedly by mistake – last time we'd been in Arakesh. Like so many things in Karazan, it didn't work quite the way you'd expect: it had started off almost completely black, areas only revealing themselves when we actually reached them. As Rich had pointed out, it was a limited amount of use only being able to see where you'd already been, instead of where you wanted to go . . . but that was Karazan for you, and a magical back-to-front map was a lot better than nothing.

Kenta rummaged inside her backpack, producing a parchment scroll, and we all shuffled closer as she fumbled for the edge to unroll it.

'Hang on a minute, Kenta,' said Jamie suddenly; 'that's the wrong one. It's not the map, it's the other parchment – the blank one.'

He was right. The parchment Kenta was unrolling was the one we'd found in the junk shop belonging to Hob's Pa. Then, it had held the cryptic clues that led us to the Temple of Serpents and the five magical potions; but it had been wiped completely clean by our re-entry into our own world months before.

But Kenta already had it half-open . . . and it wasn't blank now.

We gawked at it in silence.

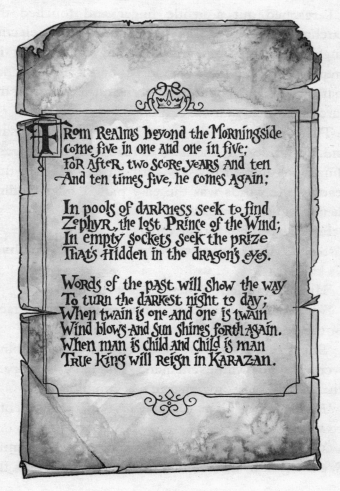

From Realms beyond the Morningside
come five in one and one in five;
For after, two score years and ten
And ten times five, he comes again;

In pools of darkness seek to find
Zephyr, the lost Prince of the Wind;
In empty sockets seek the prize
That's hidden in the dragon's eyes.

Words of the past will show the way
To turn the darkest night to day;
When twain is one and one is twain
Wind blows and Sun shines forth again.
When man is child and child is man
True King will reign in Karazan.

For what seemed a long time no one spoke.

Kai and Hob, who'd lived in Karazan all their lives, had been matter-of-fact about magic; to them, it was as everyday and ordinary as watching TV is to us. But to the five of us it was strange and wonderful, and I for one still had trouble believing it was real.

I reached out a gentle finger and touched the parchment. There it was – the unmistakable electric tingle, as if the scroll was humming softly under its breath. For a second I wondered: had it been chance that made Kenta choose the wrong one . . . or had the parchment *wanted* to be chosen?

The writing was the same as before: thick, dark and old-fashioned, and hard to read – for me, at least. But as I stumbled my way through it, I realised that reading the words was the easy part. Understanding them was totally impossible.

For me, but not for the others.

'So . . .' said Kenta slowly, 'we're *meant* to find him. Us kids – the five of us.'

'Huh?' said Rich. 'Where does it say that?'

'We must be,' said Gen, a dreamy look on her face; 'or the poem wouldn't have come to us.'

'But it actually says so, Gen!' Jamie was stumbling over his words with excitement. '*Five in one and one in five*: the *five* of us, together in *one* group!'

'*Realms beyond the Morningside* . . .' read Kenta, frowning.

'Wasn't Morningside on the map?' said Jamie. 'We'll check in a sec, but I'm sure it was! It was the area to the right of the mountains – the east, where the sun comes up – beside the Cliffs of Stone.'

'Then *realms beyond the Morningside* could mean . . . it could mean our world: the world beyond the magic portal in the Cliffs of Stone!' Gen's eyes were shining. 'That confirms beyond a doubt it's referring to us!'

'So.' Rich was scowling down at the poem as if it was a difficult sum. 'How about the next bit? *After two score years and ten.* A score's twenty, isn't it? So that makes fifty, right? And so is ten times five – fifty! They add up to the same!'

'And the *he* is . . . ' prompted Jamie.

'Zephyr!' squawked Rich.

'Exactly! Well done, Richard – see, it's not so hard after all.'

'And it ties in with what Hob told us about Zephyr coming back from exile after fifty years,' chipped in Kenta.

'The next bit tells us where to find him . . .' said Gen.

'OK, let's have a look,' said Rich, with newfound confidence. 'Yeah! How about that! It *does* tell us where to find him: *in pools of darkness!*'

'Yes – but I doubt it means it literally,' Gen objected. 'Is he really likely to be at the bottom of a dark pool, underwater?'

'Hopefully not – if he was, he'd be drowned, and that wouldn't be much good to anyone,' said Jamie with a grin.

'Look,' said Kenta. 'It goes on to talk about a *prize*

that's hidden in the dragon's eyes . . . could that also be Zephyr – the prize, I mean?'

'You don't think it could be a real dragon, do you?' asked Jamie uneasily.

'And *empty sockets* . . . what does it mean by that?'

I didn't say anything, but I had a hunch that for once I might know the answer. An image came into my mind of a matted beard and a tangled mane of hair, of a face with shrunken pouches of skin where the eyes had once been . . . Meirion, the prophet mage. But he was gone – who knew where?

'Typical Karazan,' grumbled Rich. 'If the parchment wants to tell us something, why doesn't it just do it?'

'Lucky for you Kai's not here, Richard – you'd be in for a lecture! But you're right – it is pretty cryptic, even for Karazan,' Jamie admitted.

'And that last bit's total gobbledegook, if you ask me,' Rich said, discouraged.

'Though *words of the past* could mean the things Kai and Hob told us – the legend and stuff,' said Jamie.

'There seem to be so many opposites and contradictions in that last verse,' said Kenta. 'Twain is one, wind and sun, night and day, child is man . . . it makes no sense at all.'

'It's a poem, remember,' said Jamie knowledgeably. 'Heaps of poems don't seem to make sense at first. It's because when you write one, you use a thing called poetic licence – that means you get to bend the rules a bit to make the rhythm and rhyme work out. Plus they're always full of symbolism and metaphors and stuff. So when it says, for instance, *turn night to day*, it doesn't mean it literally.'

'What does it mean then?' asked Rich.

'Well, *turn night to day* could mean . . . let me think . . . ending the dark times of King Karazeel's reign, and bringing back all the happiness and light you'd associate with good King Zane and Zephyr,' Jamie explained. 'Poetry's like that. You just have to get used to it, and then it all makes sense.'

'And one thing's for certain,' said Gen, suddenly sounding very grown-up: 'it *does* make sense. Perfect sense – just like the other magical clues. It's right here in front of us. All we need to do is figure it out.'

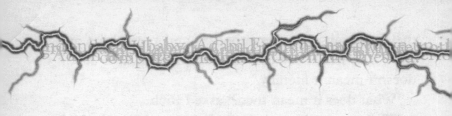

THE BOOK OF DAYS

'So,' said Rich, 'd'you reckon we look for pools of darkness, or what?'

We were huddled round the map – the right one this time – trying to decide what to do next.

'Speaking of darkness,' Gen pointed out, 'about half the map is still covered in black splodge. So the chances are that even if the pools of darkness exist, we won't know where they are till we actually get there.'

'Yeah,' I said, 'but there is one good thing about the splodge: it means we can pinpoint exactly where we are. This part of the map was covered up before, and it isn't now. We're pushing the splodge ahead of us as we move, so this –' I pointed to a kind of blunt arrowhead in the blackness – 'is where we must be.'

'That explains why the forest seems so much bigger than I remembered,' said Jamie. 'Last time we headed north, where it's narrower. But look: it stretches way further to the east . . . and for all we know, it could go on for ages.'

'But where do we go from here? I can't see any pools marked on the map – at least, not the bit we can

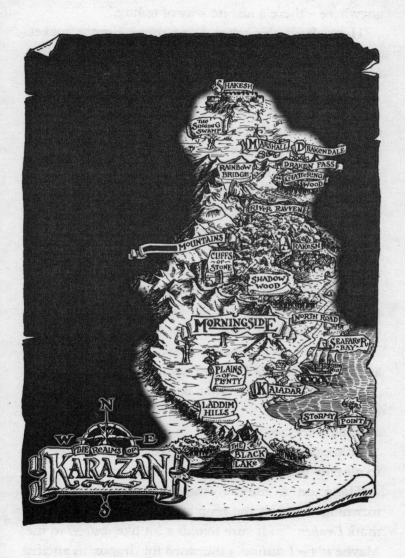

THE REALMS OF
KARAZAN

SHAKESH
THE SINGING SWAMP
MARSHALL
DRAKENDALE
RAINBOW BRIDGE
DRAKEN PASS
CHATTERING WOOD
RIVER RAVVEN
MOUNTAINS
ARAKESH
CLIFFS OF STONE
SHADOW WOOD
MORNINGSIDE
NORTH ROAD
SEAFARER BAY
PLAINS OF PLENTY
KALADAR
LADDIM HILLS
STORMY POINT
THE BLACK LAKE

N
W E
S

see,' said Kenta. 'Though as Gen says, they could be anywhere – there's just no way of telling.'

'How about the other clues then? Empty sockets . . . dragon?' hazarded Rich. 'Can anyone see, like, *Here be dragons* or anything?'

'It wouldn't mean real dragons, Richard,' said Jamie. 'Like I was saying, it's probably symbolic – or a statue of a dragon of something. And anyhow, there's no mention of dragons anywhere that I can see.'

But suddenly I noticed something – me! – and the words came tumbling out of my mouth before I had a chance to think. 'Yeah, there is! Up there in the mountains! We went through them last time, on our way to Shakesh –' I remembered a huddle of dark houses in swirling snow – 'Dragon Pass, and Dragondale!'

I grinned triumphantly round at the others. But there was something in their faces . . . I felt my smile stiffen and fade. 'What?'

'It doesn't say Dragon Pass, Adam,' said Jamie awkwardly. 'It says *Draken* Pass . . . and *Draken*dale.'

I felt my face flare. When would I learn to keep my big mouth shut – especially where reading and spelling were concerned?

'I thought it said that too, Adam,' Gen fibbed. 'It's so gloomy in here, it's hard to tell –'

'Hang on a minute, though!' Rich interrupted, frowning down at the map. 'What kind of a word is that? *Draken* . . . it sure *sounds* a lot like *dragon* to me. Maybe it's – I dunno – the word for dragon in ancient Karazanese, or something. I don't think you were wrong at all, Adam: I think you've hit the nail bang on the head.'

'You might be right. Dragon . . . draken. *Here be drakens* . . .' said Gen, trying it out.

'There's just one problem,' Rich said grimly. 'To get there, we have to cross the River Ravven again. And I don't think any of us is keen to do that.'

I felt a hollow surge of dread, and looking round at the others, I could see they felt the same. Once had been more than enough.

'There's always Rainbow Bridge.'

'But there's no guarantee it'll be sunny. And if it isn't . . .'

No rainbow. I remembered the bridge dissolving under my feet last time we'd crossed it, vanishing with the disappearing sun . . .

'Is there no other way?' I didn't realise I'd spoken aloud till Kenta answered me.

'There is – I mean, there might be. There is in the game, anyhow.' Rich gave me a half-grin and a wink; Kenta fancied herself world expert on *Quest of the Dark Citadel*. 'I've told you how long I spent trying to cross the river. Well, when I finally did, it wasn't actually the river at all. It was way over on the coast, where it joins the sea . . . I suppose you'd call it an estuary, or a delta, or something.'

'And were there . . .'

'No.' Kenta gave Gen a sympathetic little smile. 'No spiders – not even one.'

'How did you get across?' Rich asked. 'Did you swim?'

'There was a little wooden boat.' Kenta shrugged. 'I just hopped in and rowed across.'

She made it sound so easy. 'How far away is it, d'you think?' I could hear the hope in Jamie's voice.

'Well . . . it's a lot quicker walking across a computer screen than doing it in real life.' She glanced down at the map. 'But we've already gone quite a long way east . . . I'd say we'd be there by this evening, or tomorrow morning at the latest.'

'And the best part is that they won't expect us to go this way,' said Rich with satisfaction. 'Plus, a boat ride across an estuary will take care of anything that's left of our scent.' He looked round at us. 'All agreed? Come on then – what are we waiting for?'

But we didn't reach the coast by evening. When at last we emerged from the forest dusk had already fallen; the first stars were pinpricks in the evening sky, and the only sign of the sea was the faintest whiff of salt on the wind. A lonely moon hung pale on the horizon.

Far away to our left a vast lake mirrored the light of the moon like a silver bowl. A many-turreted castle rose from the water, floating on its surface like something out of one of Gen's fairy tales. 'The Dark Citadel,' said Kenta softly, 'and the lake is Stillwater. We still have a long way to go.'

Even Rich was too dog-tired to tease her. 'How

do we know old Zephyr isn't holed up in there?' he mumbled.

'Hard to see how it fits with the clues,' said Jamie.

'Could the lake be a Pool of Darkness, d'you think?' asked Gen, without much hope. But it didn't look dark to me, and none of us could summon the energy to answer her.

'I say we stop here.' The second the words were out of my mouth I saw relief flood the others' faces. 'We've done enough for one day, and there's no point trying to run on empty. How does . . . let's see . . .' I was digging through my pack, 'Creamy Potato Cheddar Soup sound – or Alpine Mashed Potato and Country Chicken with Gravy?'

'Or maybe both,' suggested Jamie, with the first real smile I'd seen for hours.

Night wrapped round our little campsite like a soft cloak. The fire had burned down to glowing embers, and the dark shapes of the others were motionless in their sleeping bags. The day had taken its toll on all of us, and as soon as the last plate of steaming stew had been scraped clean all anyone could think of was sleep. When Rich reluctantly mumbled something about 'first watch' there'd been a deafening silence – but unlike the others I didn't feel at all tired. Physically, yes – I was stiff and sore from my fall down the stone steps, and my legs felt like lead after the frantic dash through the forest and the hours of walking – but my mind was in overdrive.

I felt for my ring, meaning to thread it onto its bootlace and hang it back round my neck. Took it out and held it for a moment, watching the way it seemed to draw silvery light from the moon and the distant water. And suddenly I ached to play my penny whistle. I could hear the exact sequence of notes in my mind, crystal clear as the ripples of moonlight on water. But I didn't want to wake the others.

Restlessly I stood and strode over to my pack. I could work out the fingering, at least . . . I reached into my bag, my fingers feeling for the smoothness of metal; but instead they met the soft texture of leather. I drew out the little book – the *Book of Days* – and walked slowly back to my log. Still hearing the song of my flute in my head, I absently opened the cover again, half-wondering what could be so precious about an empty book that it should be kept so secret . . .

Then the moonlight fell on the dark page, and the music in my mind stopped as abruptly as a radio being snapped off.

There was writing where there had been only emptiness before. A graceful, flowing, cursive script, written in glowing mother-of-pearl that shone out from the parchment like starlight. Hardly daring to breathe in case it disappeared, I managed to decipher the first few words:

I am Princess Zaronel of Antarion. I write in moonlight, words to be read on some moonlit night far hence, by whom I do not know . . .

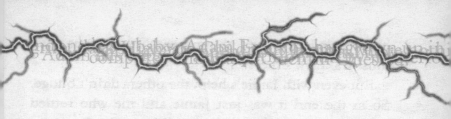

WORDS OF THE PAST

I was up in a flash and over at the sleeping shape of Rich, shaking him none too gently by the shoulder. 'Hey, Rich – wake up! That book: there's writing in it! *Richard!*'

'Garrawazza . . . flumblepish . . .' mumbled Rich, turned over and started to snore.

I tried the girls, but they didn't so much as twitch. Without much hope I crouched down beside Jamie and gave him a poke with my finger. 'Jamie,' I hissed. 'Jamie! Wake up! There's writing in the book – you can read it by moonlight!'

Jamie's eyes popped open and he sat up like a jack-in-the-box. 'Honest? How cool is that! Let me see . . .' He reached out his hand for the book and rapidly scanned the first page. Then he looked up at me again, his face very solemn. 'D'you realise how important this is, Adam? It could be the key to every-thing. It's a diary, belonging to Zaronel before she was made queen . . . the *words of the past* the poem talks about! It'll tell us what happened to Prince Zephyr, and where to find him – it has to!' He struggled out of his sleeping bag, eyes shining with excitement. 'We must wake the others!'

But even with Jamie's help, the others didn't budge. So in the end it was just Jamie and me who settled ourselves in our sleeping bags with our backs to my log and a mug of cocoa each, toes stretched out to the fire. 'Shall I read it out loud?' Jamie offered. 'I'm real good at reading grown-up writing.' Without waiting for an answer, he wiggled himself into a more comfortable position, took a noisy slurp of cocoa, and began.

I am Princess Zaronel of Antarion. I write in moonlight, words to be read on some moonlit night far hence, by whom I do not know.

This Book of Days was given to me by my father as a parting gift, and the quill by my mother. Though it looks at first sight to be a silver arrowhead, it draws out into a finely-crafted feather whose magical filaments pull the moonbeams from the night sky onto the page before me.

It is strange to think that these same two moons shine down upon Antarion, many long days' journey across the sea. How I long for home . . . to be in my own familiar chamber, instead of this lonely turret room so far away!

They call me the Jewel of Antarion, and a jewel I am indeed: a thing of no real worth, a mere trinket to be bartered in the game of power. Had I been born a prince, I would be free to ride astride and wield a sword . . . and free to be king after my father. But now the future of Antarion depends upon this alliance with Karazan; though I have but sixteen summers, I must wed a stranger and hope that one day I will bear a son to rule the united empire.

At sunrise I must prepare for an audience with the Princes of Karazan. Prince Zane and Prince Zeel . . . I do not know which I will be forced to wed, nor do I care.

The choice will not be mine to make. According to the tradition of Karazan, a contest will be held to decide which of the princes will ascend the throne; I must marry the one chosen as king.

In the three days before the contest the princes will pay court to me, each day presenting me with a gift of their own choosing. But I care nothing for them or their gifts, no matter how lavish they may be! I am sick to my heart for home. All I take comfort from is Zagros, the companion of my childhood, pledged to protect me until I choose to send him hence.

But he is all I have to remind me of Antarion – and I shall keep him here forever!

'Imagine that,' said Jamie after a pause. 'Sent to a strange land, forced to marry someone you've never even met – and having to worry about babies and stuff when you're only sixteen! That's the end of the first entry – it carries on over the page.' He took a long swallow of cocoa, and made a face. 'Yuck – this has gone cold. Adam . . . it's weird. The diary's written in old-fashioned language, so you'd think it'd be hard to understand. But it isn't. I can see it all so clearly, can't you? I've always imagined Queen Zaronel really beautiful; a bit like Gen, with long, wavy golden hair.' He blushed in the darkness, and shot me a quick sidelong glance to check I wasn't laughing at him.

'Go on,' I said, though I knew what he was going to say.

'But now, reading this, I can see her sitting at the window writing – a tall, narrow window with a curved top, a shaft of moonlight falling on the page. Her long hair is falling round her shoulders, but it's not golden: it's dark, almost black, and her eyes are grey as mist . . .'

'You're seeing it the way it really was,' I said slowly. 'I saw it too. The *Book of Days* . . . it's more than just a diary, Jamie. It's a window to the past, in a way I don't even begin to understand.'

Jamie gave me the smallest of smiles. In the glow of the firelight he looked somehow different from his usual chubby, baby-faced self. 'You're right,' he said softly. 'It's called magic, I guess.' Smiling back, I was suddenly glad it was Jamie who'd woken, and not Rich or Kenta or Gen.

Then Jamie turned the page and read on, the words of the past swirling round us both like dark water, drawing us down deep and deeper still, back to those long-ago days . . . and once again I saw the events unfolding in my mind as Jamie read Zaronel's words, as clearly as if I'd actually been there.

Zaronel was woken by a soft tap on the heavy wooden door. She had closed the shutters of the tall window before

*she fell asleep, and the room was dark and the air brittle
with cold.*

*The door opened a crack and the young maidservant
Karris peeped shyly in. 'It is time for you to rise, my
lady,' she said with a little bob. 'May I enter and make up
the fire?'*

*'Of course.' Zaronel settled back into the softness of the
furs and watched as the maid crouched at the stone fire-
place, arranging firewood with nimble fingers. In moments
the room was filled with crackling warmth.*

'It has snowed in the night, my lady.'

*Yes – that was the chill that had made its way through
the stone walls! Instantly Zaronel was out of bed and
throwing open the casement. Icy air rushed in, stinging
her cheeks and bringing tears to her eyes. Everything was
carpeted in white . . . the trees wore mantles of ermine . . .*

*'Come away from the window, my lady! You will catch
your death of cold!'*

*'No I won't!' Zaronel laughed. 'The first snows never
hurt anybody, Karris – and see how beautiful it is! Oh,
how I wish I could saddle a horse and ride out this
morning, instead of . . .' She bit her lip, a shadow falling
over her face as she gazed down at the snow.*

*She did not feel the maidservant tuck a soft wrap round
her shoulders, or hear her bustling round the chamber,
poking the fire till the sparks flew, pouring water, setting
out the gown she was to wear for her first audience with
the princes.*

I will face whatever lies ahead without flinching,
Zaronel told herself, for the sake of Antarion. *But her*

heart felt as heavy and cold as a stone under her silken nightdress.

Just as she was about to turn back to the room, a movement at the edge of the forest caught her eye. A man on horseback. The horse was as magnificent as any Zaronel had ever seen, even in her father's court: a winged stallion the colour of fire, power and energy harnessed to a perfect partnership with the rider.

Zaronel watched, entranced, as the horse paced proudly out from the trees . . . and then a hare leapt out from almost under its hooves. Instantly the stallion exploded, corkscrewing sideways, then leaping forward and throwing out his wings to take flight. Zaronel gasped, expecting to see the rider crash to the ground . . . but he sat light and easy in the saddle, his perfect balance seeming to anticipate the horse's every movement. In seconds the stallion was collected again, neck arched and steam snorting from his nostrils as he danced forward, printing an even chain of hoof-prints in the new snow.

Now Zaronel's attention was on the rider, not the horse. Some servant, sent out in the chill dawn to exercise a mount that could only belong to a nobleman. He was bareheaded, wearing the homespun breeches of a commoner and a worn leather jerkin. He held the reins in one hand; the other arm cradled something swathed in the folds of his cloak. Zaronel smiled. A brace of conies, no doubt, poached from the royal forest. But he rides like no man I have ever seen . . .

At that moment, passing below the tower, the man glanced up. For a second their eyes met: the wide grey eyes

150

of the princess, clasping the shawl to her breast, her heart suddenly quickening . . . the clear hazel eyes of the horseman, beneath a rough tangle of hair the rich red-brown of autumn leaves.

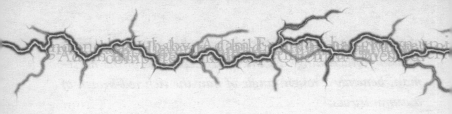

JAMIE'S SECRET

I rubbed my eyes, blinking stupidly into the fire as the pictures I'd seen so vividly in the glowing embers wavered and faded into the shadows. Somehow, the night seemed to have darkened . . .

I looked up. The sky that had been so clear when Jamie started reading was streaked with tattered cloud blowing in from the sea. The moon was a blurry smudge, and the stars had almost disappeared.

Jamie was squinting down at the book, his nose just about touching the page. 'It's no good,' he said regretfully. 'The writing's gone.'

'Perhaps it's just as well. We really ought to wait and read it with the others, in case we miss something.'

Jamie closed the book and handed it back to me, yawning. 'Anyway, I'm tired.' He stood, still in his sleeping bag, and sack-jumped a couple of hops further from the fire. 'Are you OK to keep watch still, Adam?'

'Yeah,' I said. 'I'm fine.' The restlessness I'd felt earlier had been replaced by the slightly dazed, spaced-out feeling you get when you've been reading for too long and have lost track of time.

Jamie settled down with his hands behind his head, staring up at the sky. I took a couple more logs from the pile and criss-crossed them on the fire, watching the flames turn purple and send out tiny yellow tongues to lick at the wood.

As the fire flared up, the surrounding darkness deepened. I was about to go over to my pack to find my penny whistle when Jamie spoke again, almost too softly to hear. 'I reckon she's in love.'

'What?' He'd curled over onto his side like a fat caterpillar and was staring at me, eyes wide and solemn-looking. 'Who?'

'Princess Zaronel. She's come to Karazan to marry one of the princes, but now she's fallen in love with the guy on the horse. What will she do, d'you think?' A pause; then: 'Do you believe in love at first sight, Adam?'

Only Jamie could start with that kind of stuff in the middle of the night. 'Nah,' I growled, scowling into the fire. 'I don't even know if I believe in love, full stop.'

'Well, I bet you didn't believe in magic either, till you came to Karazan.'

He had me there. I shrugged.

'*I* do.'

'That's great, Jamie. I'm happy for you. Go to sleep.'

'Adam . . . have you ever . . . *liked* someone?'

'Sure I have. I like you guys – and I've got this friend called Cameron . . .'

'That's not what I mean.'

'Jamie,' I said, trying to make my whisper sound impatient enough to shut him up, 'we've got a long day ahead. I really think –'

'Have you ever been out with anyone – a girl, I mean?'

An uncomfortable memory glooped slowly up from the depths of my subconscious like a glob in a lava lamp. A couple of months ago there'd been a rash of boy-girl stuff at school. Suddenly everyone was 'going out' with everyone else . . . everyone except me. It was all anyone talked about. Even Cam persuaded me to take a message to Nicole's best friend asking if Nicole wanted to go out with him – and she'd said yes, coke-bottle specs and all. To hear old Cam talk, it was the romance of the century. They spent every break time in the library, sitting opposite each other at the table in the corner, noses deep in their books. Far as I know, they never actually exchanged a single word.

Then I got this letter. I found it in my desk one morning when I arrived at school – right there on top of my dictionary. A piece of yellow paper with a tiny bluebird in the corner, folded in half. *Adam Equinox*, it said on the front; so I knew for sure it was meant for me. I could tell at once it was written by a girl. The writing was round and curvy, with a little circle instead of a dot on top of the 'i'.

I snatched it up and stuffed it into my pocket and headed off to the boys' toilet, red as a beetroot. Locked myself into a cubicle, closed the lid and sat down. Stood up again, fished out the letter; sat down again. Stared at it. *Adam Equinox.*

One thing was for sure: it *was* from a girl. Another thing – for certain sure – it really was for me. I opened it out with numb, clumsy fingers. The writing was big and round and easy to read.

I think you're cute. Interested? Then meet me at the drinking fountain by the art room at break. C U there – I hope! Christie

After the *Christie* was an X – more of an x really, I guess; small and tidy, with a circle round it.

I knew what that X meant.

Cute . . . me? And for it to be from Christie Martin . . . As far as I could tell, she didn't even know I existed. She was part of this ultra-cool group of girls – not *part* of it: the centre of it. They didn't play at break time; instead they wandered round watching the other kids with disdainful looks on their faces, nudging each other and giggling. Or they'd sit in a huddle on one of the circular benches under the trees, doing whatever it is girls do.

Christie . . . she was tall – almost as tall as me – with white-blonde hair so straight it looked like she ironed it. She had one of those cool, haughty faces that would be pretty if it ever smiled; she wore her skirt kind of hiked up to show off her long brown legs. Every time I ever got close to her – pushing past to

the lockers, say – she had this way of glancing sideways and kind of tossing her hair that made me feel
like dirt.

And now . . .

I couldn't get my head round it. I sat like I'd been
turned to stone till long after the bell, staring at the
note. Stumbled into class late with a mumbled excuse
to the McCracken . . . risked a quick look over at
Christie's desk by the door, thinking maybe she'd give
me a smile or a wink or some kind of a sign. But she
just carried on marking her homework without so
much as glancing up.

Cam rushed off to the library as soon as the
bell went, specs misted over with passion. The other
guys grabbed a softball and bat and disappeared in
the direction of the playing field. As for me . . . I
slouched past the science lab to the art room and
skulked outside, trying to look like I just happened to
be passing.

After ten minutes, I wondered if I'd read the note
wrong.

After twenty, I was about ready to leave.

After half an hour, break time was over.

I walked into class with my eyes glued to the floor
. . . past Christie's desk to mine, up front under the
McCracken's watchful eye.

A ripple of giggles followed me to my seat. I pulled
out my chair, scowling like fury, ears on fire. From
behind me I heard a sweeter-than-sugar whisper:
'Enjoy your break, Adam?'

I didn't hate them for doing it; I hated myself for believing it.

Now I tuned back in to Jamie. Turned out he hadn't waited for an answer; he was burbling on, seemingly more interested in talking than listening. 'But of course I'd die if anyone found out, even her. *Especially* her. Do you absolutely promise never to tell anyone, Adam?'

'Huh?' I was totally lost. 'Who are you talking about?'

'You know who! I've just been telling you!'

Blankly, I tried to rewind a conversation I hadn't heard a word of. Why was he rambling on like this – why now, and why to me? But I knew he'd be hurt if he realised I hadn't been listening to a thing he'd said . . . 'Don't you worry, Jamie – your secret's safe with me,' I said gruffly, man to man. Couldn't be safer, I thought wryly.

But Jamie wasn't finished yet.

'It's like the other person's way more important to you than you are yourself . . . you know you'd do *anything* for that person – absolutely anything, without a second thought. Haven't you ever felt that way about anyone, Adam?'

I pretended to think about it. Truth was, I was way out of my league in this mysterious one-sided conversation. Then suddenly a picture popped into my head – but it wasn't Christie Martin, or anyone remotely like her. It was old bossy-boots Hannah Quested with

157

her dandelion hair and sparkly smile – all five years old of her. I couldn't help grinning in the dark. Yeah, I had to admit I'd turn myself upside-down and inside-out to see that cheeky little smile – but that wasn't what Jamie was talking about. 'Nah,' I said, 'not so you'd notice. I guess I really just don't do romance.

'And now, Jamie, for goodness sake turn over and go to sleep!'

A PIECE OF CAKE

We left Stillwater behind us in the cool dawn, its still surface reflecting the pink and gold of the rising sun.

On and on we tramped, expecting any minute to see the glint of the sea. But the sun was high in the sky and hot on our shoulders before we finally crested a low rise and there it was in front of us: blinding blue stretching away to the curve of the horizon, low lines of surf furling in to spread themselves on a level beach of sun-washed sand.

To our left was the river. Kenta had told us the estuary was a wide unbroken expanse of water. And it would be – at high tide. But now the river met the sea in a shallow, sprawling fan, twisted ribbons of water winding their way between flat spits of sand.

'The river's tidal,' Jamie told us knowledgeably. 'I'll bet that's why the water spiders aren't a problem here – the water's salty so close to the sea.'

'Well, we aren't going to be able to row across, that's for sure,' Rich said cheerfully, 'even though Kenta's famous boat's there – look!' Sure enough, on our side of the river, high and dry and looking as though it hadn't been used in years, a small wooden rowing boat lay on its side. 'But the good news is, we won't need to. See how flat the beach is, and how quickly the tide's going out? I bet by the time we get down to the water we'll be able to walk across without even getting our feet wet!'

Rich was right. Even in the short time we'd been standing there, the sea had retreated a good distance.

We grinned round at each other. But then Gen spoke up, a peculiar wobble in her voice. 'I don't know . . . I don't like this river, Richard. We know Kenta made the crossing safely in the boat; I think we should wait till the tide comes up again and do it her way. I keep remembering last time at the ford, those spiders . . . the River Ravven's evil, even here, close to the sea.'

Rich rolled his eyes impatiently. 'Oh, twaddle! I say we've really struck it lucky. If crossing in the boat was easy, walking across is going to be a doddle. What d'you think, Kenta? You're the expert!'

Kenta gave Gen's shoulder a squeeze. 'I know how you feel, Gen,' she said apologetically, 'but the river truly is different down here. Look at it: it's almost disappeared, and what's left is slow and shallow and safe.'

'Yeah – they're just trickles, and most of them look narrow enough to hop over!' agreed Jamie. 'How about we all go down and have a look, Gen? We'll check out the boat, and make sure there isn't any sign of . . . anything . . . in the water.'

Less than half an hour later we were standing in a semi-circle round the boat, surveying it gloomily. From a distance it had looked a bit weatherworn, but seaworthy enough. Now we could see that the caulking that had once sealed its joints had shrunk and fallen away in places, leaving cracks that would let water through in moments. If that wasn't bad enough, one splintery-looking oar lay half-buried in the sand close by, and there was no sign of the other.

'Well,' said Rich with satisfaction, 'so much for your boat, Kenta.' He flopped down on the sand and pulled one boot off, wrinkling his nose and grinning up at us. 'Don't know about you guys, but I wouldn't say no to a paddle – these feet sure could do with a wash!'

With a sigh of relief I sank down under the shade of a cluster of strange-looking plants. They had thick succulent stems, topped with stiff circular leaves the size of elephants' ears. At high tide I guessed they'd float on the surface like water lilies, but now they reared up from the dry riverbank like huge umbrellas. Away on the other side of the estuary I could see more of them, far-off clusters of polka dots on the gently sloping shore.

I tugged my boots off and peeled off my socks, stuffing them into my backpack. Glancing up, I saw that Jamie had padded down to the water in his bare feet, and was turning to call back to us. 'It's clear as anything and real shallow, Gen – I can see right to the bottom. There's nothing to worry about!'

161

I stood, hefted my pack, and walked over to join him. He was right: the dark, oily-looking water that had made the river seem so menacing at the ford was crystal-clear and sparkling. The close-packed sand, fine as powder, felt cool and soothing under the aching soles of my feet. Tentatively, I dipped one toe into the water: it was cold as ice, like liquid glass.

'Ten minutes tops, I reckon,' said Rich heartily. 'Like I said: a piece of cake.'

As he said the words, a sudden, sickening qualm of foreboding swept through me: a feeling like vertigo, as if I was teetering on a cliff-edge about to plummet into darkness.

'Wait a sec, Rich.' He turned back, frowning. The others had already started picking their way across the sand.

I hesitated. The lurch of dread was fading to a niggling unease. Had I imagined it? 'Guys – wait up a moment!' They stopped obediently, exchanging puzzled glances. I raised my hand to my forehead to block the dazzle and gazed slowly round me, turning full circle. Out over the estuary, where rivulets of water caught the sun between smooth dun-coloured sandbanks. Back to the bank, scuffmarks showing where we'd sat to take our shoes off, the flat umbrella-plants motionless in the still air. Out towards the sea, a distant bar of brightness beyond the vast emptiness of sand, the murmur of waves almost too faint to hear.

That was it. The tide. Richard had been right: here at the river mouth the ground was almost completely flat. The tide that had run out so swiftly would come back in like an express train; once it turned, the sea would flood the estuary in minutes.

And we had no way of knowing when that would be.

But like Rich had said, ten minutes tops and we'd be safely over. And even if the tide did catch us, the worst that would happen was we'd have an unscheduled swim. The longer I dithered . . . With a last quick check in the direction of the distant sea, I followed the others out onto the sand.

Close to the bank, the surface of the river bed was firm and almost dry. Here and there, shallow pools of water were completely surrounded by sand, stranded by the falling tide. But it wasn't long before I came to the first of the long strands of water that had found softer sand, carving their way through to the sea. Ahead of me, Rich had already splashed his way across, turning to grin and give a thumbs-up to Jamie and the girls. I waded across after him, enjoying the crisp feel of the cold water on my sweaty feet.

As we neared the centre of the river bed the runnels of water became wider and deeper. Though my breeches were rolled up to my knees, the bunched cloth was soon soaked. I guessed it made sense that the current – what there was of it – would be stronger towards the middle; but even here, the water was nowhere near deep enough for even Gen to worry about. Still, I gave a quick glance over my shoulder to check she was OK; she was sloshing along happily with the hem of her ragged tunic bunched in one hand to keep it dry, the other splashing a sparkling spray of water at Jamie. I shook my head, grinning: so much for Gen's evil River Ravven!

By now we'd spread out into a relaxed straggle. Rich was up ahead, apparently trying to prove his claim about wet feet by jumping over as many of the streams as possible; I could hear him counting to himself after every clumsy leap. Over on my left was Kenta; Jamie was lagging behind, trudging round the pools of water rather than through them, picking his way cautiously through the streams. Away on his right and closest to the sea was Gen, fossicking happily along like a kid at the seaside.

The shore was close now. I waded through the last wide rivulet, savouring the cool tickle of ripples on my skin and the suck of wet sand between my toes. I could make out lanky long-legged wading birds poking round among the grasses on the bank; above us grey gulls wheeled and called.

Rich was right, I thought. *It is a piece of cake. There was nothing to worry about.*

That was when Gen screamed.

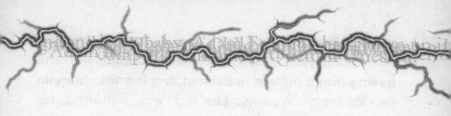

ABSOLUTELY ANYTHING

It was a single wavering shriek of raw terror.

I spun round. Gen was standing on a broad flat sandbar between two streams. She was stock-still, arms in the air as if she'd frozen in the middle of some kind of dance. Her eyes were huge and staring.

I drew a shaky breath to call out to her – something – I didn't know what. But before I could make a sound her whole body gave a weird, twitching spasm.

Her feet were buried in the sand. When she moved – a convulsive side-to-side swaggering motion, hands clutching uselessly at nothing – she somehow seemed to slip. Instantly, she froze into immobility again, panting.

'What the . . .' Rich, behind me, amusement and a hint of worry in his voice.

I stared, my mind refusing to take in what I was seeing. Before, her feet had been buried; now, she was almost knee-deep in sand.

The truth smacked me in the face like an icy wave. Suddenly everything seemed to be happening in slow motion and complete silence. Jamie was running towards her. His feet kicked up a glittering spray of water with each stride, flat sheets fanning out and fraying into a million individual droplets that hung in the air for an eternity. His face was contorted, his mouth moving, no words coming out.

Rich's harsh shout snapped me back into real time. 'Jamie – stay away from there! Gen – don't struggle. Just . . . just keep still . . .'

Rich was beside me now, but I couldn't force my legs to move . . . couldn't wrench my eyes away from Gen. Her face was unrecognisable; she wasn't the Gen I knew. She was trapped in her fear like an animal, her eyes staring sightlessly out of her white face, fixed on something none of us could see. She gave a tiny whimper, like a puppy . . . then another desperate struggling lurch that buried her thigh-deep.

At last, I started to run.

Jamie was in the water in front of her now, holding out his hands . . . but it was too far, way too far to reach. He was mumbling something, over and over again. Gen reached out her arms to him, fingers straining. The space between them yawned like an abyss.

Then she spoke: two words, whispered on the faintest breath. '*Help me . . .*'

Without hesitation Jamie stumbled forward. One step . . . two . . . three . . . Their hands clasped. Jamie heaved like someone in a tug-of-war. For a long moment Gen seemed to stretch as the grip of the quicksand loosened. Then Jamie's feet shuffled in a staggering quick-step as he struggled for footing in the quaking sand . . . and his face melted into terror as the solid sand gave way to a sucking nothingness.

He threw himself backwards. At first I thought it was a frantic effort to escape the grip of the sand, but then I saw he'd pulled Gen with him. She was lying half on top of him, clutching onto him with the desperate strength of panic.

'Gen – crawl – pull yourself up on me . . .' Jamie gasped. '*Do it!*' Gen's hands clawed at him; eyes wild with terror, she grabbed at his jerkin, dragging herself out of the mire and up onto his body.

'Spread out your arms, Jamie!' I heard myself shouting. 'Spread your legs, if you can – it'll stop you sinking . . .' . . . *as fast.* Rich and I were close now, sludgy slime between our toes . . . close enough to see how deep Gen's extra weight had already pushed Jamie into the sand.

Sobbing and gasping, Gen crawled up Jamie's chest till she was level with his face. His head was half-buried, but he gave her a tiny smile of encouragement that almost broke my heart. 'Go on, Gen,' he whispered. 'You're almost there. I'll get out easy once you're safe.'

I threw down my cloak and flung myself onto it, feeling the ground shift and quiver beneath me. 'Rich – my ankles! Gen – grab my hands! *Quick!*'

With a whimper, Gen crept forward onto the sand. For a second I thought she'd made it – but I couldn't reach her. I wriggled forward like a snake, Rich's

167

hands like steel bands on my ankles; felt the ground give under the fabric of the cloak . . . then Gen's fingers were gripping mine tight enough to crush them. 'Rich – *now!*' For a second I felt like my arms were being wrenched out of the sockets; then, with a slither and a sob, Gen was beside me on dry sand.

'Kenta –' But Kenta didn't need telling. She was there already, her dry cloak at the ready, enclosing Gen in her arms.

Panting, I turned back to Jamie. He seemed impossibly far away. His head was towards us, face-up. His ears were under, his neck, chin, most of his hair . . . the sand was at the corners of his eyes. They were staring upwards at the sky; I realised the gulls were still there, circling and calling. As I watched, Jamie's eyes rolled to meet mine with an expression I couldn't begin to read. Below the moon face, his tummy bulged like a round island. Further down his toes stuck up, two rows of little pink mushrooms sprouting out of the sand.

'At least he doesn't seem to be sinking much, now that Gen . . .' Rich was muttering. 'I reckon there's time to –'

'Adam. Richard.' It was Kenta. She spoke quietly, but there was something in her voice . . .

Was Gen . . . I turned. Gen was huddled safe in the cloak, her head cradled in her arms. But Kenta – Kenta was pointing. I followed the direction of her hand . . . and my heart stopped.

A endless sheet of gleaming water was creeping

towards us. Rhythmic ripples edged with froth slid across the sand in a stealthy moonwalk, each wavelet sneaking over the next to bring the sea closer, then closer still.

I'd been wrong. The sea wasn't coming in like an express train.

It was coming in like the tide: silent, unstoppable, deadly.

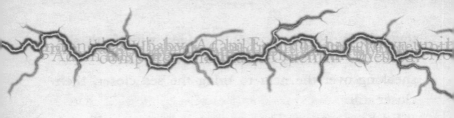

JAMIE

I tore my eyes away from the water and back to Jamie. 'Wh-what is it?' he quavered. 'What have you seen?'

I imagined how he must feel – lying trapped and totally helpless, seeing the dawning horror on our faces . . .

I glanced at Rich. He gave his head a tiny shake. I knew what he was trying to say. If we told Jamie the truth he'd panic for sure – start struggling, and . . . Better to make up some soothing lie. But Jamie didn't deserve a lie – not now, after what he'd done for Gen. If Jamie was in deadly danger, he deserved to know the truth – and be given the chance to deal with it in his own way.

'Remember to keep still,' I told him, my voice level and unemotional. 'It's the tide, Jamie – the tide is coming in.'

Jamie's face seemed to somehow sag. He closed his eyes for a moment. When he spoke, it was in a whisper I could hardly hear. 'H-how far . . .'

'Oh, it's way away still –' said Rich airily, glaring at me.

'Not far.' And then suddenly, seeing him lying there, small and brave and utterly helpless, I knew I couldn't – wouldn't – let it happen. The River Ravven wasn't going to get any of us – not Gen, not Jamie – not now, not ever. 'Don't worry, Jamie – we're going to get you out.' It was true. *I'd make it be*.

But there wasn't a second to lose.

My cloak lay between me and Jamie, damp and dinted, already almost submerged in the sand. It had held my weight while I pulled Gen over the sand – just. There was no way it would carry the combined weight of Rich and me – and to free Jamie, deep as he was, we'd both need to be right beside him. But if we were, we'd sink.

We needed something solid to stand on. Something flat and rigid . . . planks of wood . . . the boat? But it was too far away across the sand . . . and the sea had almost reached us.

Sleeping bags? Our packs? There was nothing . . .

Jamie gave the tiniest whimper. The sea was lapping at his toes.

Frantically I turned full circle, scanning the shore for something, anything, we could use – and then I was running, shouting over my shoulder for Rich and Kenta to follow me. Leaping across the sand – hurdling the remaining rivulets, now flowing strongly with the returning tide – bounding up the bank. I raced to the nearest clump of umbrella plants and grabbed one. Took hold of the stem just below the leaf, wrenched and twisted . . . it bent and cracked, pale greenish sap oozing out onto my hand. The huge flat leaf flopped over, but the stem was tough and fibrous and wouldn't come away. I yanked at the fibres, trying to snap them, but instead of breaking they split down the stem . . . I tore at them, cursing. Then Rich was beside me, pocket knife in hand. One swipe, two, and the leaf toppled to the ground. Instantly we were on to the next, the next and the next – how many would we need?

'That's it – it has to be! There's no more time!'

The leaves were huge and slippery and weighed a ton. We threw them into a pile and hefted it, the three of us staggering under its weight. Slid back down the bank and tottered over the sand at a stumbling run, reeling like drunks, water splashing under our feet with every stride.

Then Gen was there to help us, throwing down the leaves like giant green stepping stones, paving the way to Jamie. His wispy blond hair was floating now, like some kind of bizarre sea anemone; his eyes were closed, and his face wore a strange, peaceful expression.

If the leaves held, well and good; if they didn't, too bad. We'd all go down with Jamie. We ran onto them, feeling them settle onto the sand through the sheet of water. I dropped to my knees, digging frantically through the sucking wetness for Jamie's hand. Across from me, Rich was doing the same; Gen dug under Jamie's head and lifted it so he could breathe – for the moment at least. With every second, the water was deeper.

Suddenly I felt something cold and lifeless as a dead fish – grabbed it. Staggered upright, feeling the leaf tilt; heaved. Rich was on his feet and heaving too; Gen and Kenta had Jamie's head well clear now, pushing on his exposed shoulders for all they were worth.

And then it was over. The river gave Jamie up, the quicksand releasing him with a popping slurp like marrow being sucked from a bone. Sobbing and gasping, we half-dragged, half-carried him to shore.

I looked back over my shoulder – once. A smooth sheet of water covered the estuary, reflecting the blue sky and a couple of wispy clouds. A forlorn scatter of waterlily pads drifted aimlessly, turning on the tide. I had a momentary vision of what might have been . . . of Jamie's face cold and serene under the water, his hair wafting like seaweed in the rising tide.

I remembered how he'd spoken to me last night, the things he'd said. Now finally I understood what he had been talking about. And I wondered . . . had he had some kind of premonition that something would happen today – a premonition of how close he would come . . .

We turned our backs on the River Ravven and walked northwards until we were well out of sight of the estuary. Here we turned inland, the hiss and sigh of the sea fading to a whisper and then to nothing, our clothes drying gradually in the heat of the sun.

I felt an odd shyness with the others, as if we'd brushed too close to something none of us understood; come too close to looking into the eyes of something dark and nameless that would have changed us all forever.

We walked on past lunchtime, through the long afternoon and into the twilight. At last the purple shades of evening blended into the deeper darkness of trees and we slowed and stopped, reaching for water bottles and hunting for the map.

'I think we're on the eastern edge of Chattering Wood,' said Rich, squinting down at it in the gathering gloom. 'What say we stop here for the night? We're close enough to the forest to gather firewood, but hopefully safe from the chatterbots out here in the open. And we're well out of sight of the north road.'

My legs were wooden with tiredness. Poor Jamie was grey and staggering, the girls pale, pinch-faced and swaying. Only Richard was cheerful and full of energy, laying and lighting the fire practically single-handed and chivvying us all along with bad jokes and promises of a gourmet meal.

But hot food and the bright cheer of the fire worked their usual magic, and by bedtime our exhaustion had given way to a feeling of weary wellbeing.

'Look at that moon,' murmured Gen, gazing up at the silvery sky. 'The diary – shall we see if the magic you told us about works again?'

I dug it out from the depths of my pack and handed it across to her. She opened it, and her face lit up with excitement. 'Yes! It's there – the writing . . .' Jamie and I had told the others what we'd read the night before; now Gen leafed eagerly through the first few pages before looking up at us with shining eyes. 'I think this must be where you read to, Jamie – shall I go on?'

Her soft voice began to read. The night around us seemed to tremble and dissolve, and once again the words of the past wove their spell on us all . . . and as Gen gave voice to Zaronel's words from long ago, we were transported back into the past, watching her story unfold before our eyes.

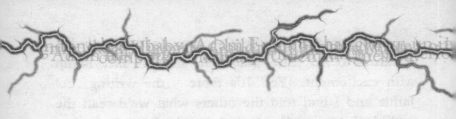

THE THREE GIFTS

*T*he red carpet running the length of the great throne room was lined with heralds in the scarlet and golden livery of the Royal House of Karazan. Each held a silver trumpet in one hand and a furled standard in the other.

At one end of the carpet were the vast studded double doors through which the princes were to enter. At the other was the throne, empty as it had been since the death of the old king two moons before. On its seat, on a velvet cushion tasselled with gold, rested the Twisted Crown of Karazan – plain gold and silver interlocking bands, unadorned with gems of any kind – and the Sign of Sovereignty.

Zaronel was seated on an ornately-carved chair to one side of the throne. In accordance with Karazan custom she wore a simple gown of white, signifying purity. Her dark hair was intertwined with flowers – the last of the autumn, in shades of scarlet and gold.

Half a pace behind her stood a figure in the bronze breastplate and crested helm of Antarion, one hand on his sword-hilt. Zagros, Guardian of the Jewel of Antarion.

At an invisible signal, fifty trumpets were raised and

176

fifty flags unfurled to show the royal emblem of twin moons encircled by a twisted crown. A clarion rang out. As the last echoes died away, the double doors were flung open and a figure in black stood framed in the archway, eyes fixed on Princess Zaronel.

'His Imperial Highness Crown Prince Zeel of Karazan!'

Zaronel watched as Prince Zeel strode forward, glancing neither left nor right. At last he reached the first of the three low steps that led to her dais and gave a low bow.

There was no doubt that Prince Zeel was handsome. Pale, hooded eyes; black hair drawn back and bound after the fashion of the nobility of Karazan. Olive skin, smooth-shaven and unlined. But there was something about the emptiness of his eyes and the curve of his mouth that sent a chill through Zaronel's heart.

She forced herself to smile and extended a hand. 'My lord . . .' Her voice, though soft, carried to every corner of the waiting hall.

He straightened, stepped forward and raised her hand to his lips. Though her flesh shrank from the touch of his skin and the heat of his breath, her face showed nothing. 'You are welcome to the court of Karazan,' he said smoothly, his lips curling into a practised smile. 'I come in quest of your hand, Zaronel of Antarion. I pray you accept this humble gift.'

Two pages hurried forward with a gilt table. On it lay a fur more magnificent than any Zaronel had ever seen. It was whiter than the snow, deep and luxuriant . . . she ran her hand through it, and it was like touching a cloud.

'For many moons my hunters searched the northernmost reaches of Karazan for the cubs of the snow wolf. For your pleasure they were tracked over the uncharted snowfields; for your delight each last one was slaughtered. Accept this mantle as token of my suit, and wear it well.'

Zaronel felt the blood drain from her face, and a wave of dizziness swept over her. 'Forgive me.' She opened her eyes, forcing her voice to be steady. 'I thank you for your gift, Prince Zeel.'

The table was moved aside, and once again the trumpets sang out. But before the fanfare finished a man was striding towards her, and in moments they were face to face. Zaronel did not hear the herald announce Crown Prince Zane of Karazan; did not remember a lifetime of being taught that a lady never stares.

Before her stood a tall young man, broad-chested and long-limbed. A wide forehead; level brows; eyes that met her own with disturbing directness. A mouth too wide to be handsome, with a kink of humour at its corner. A strong, square chin . . . a flat-planed jaw with the sandpaper roughness of beard . . . hair damp and hastily combed, the colour of autumn leaves.

In his arms he held the cloak he had been wearing earlier, wrapped in an untidy bundle. He cradled it with exaggerated care, as if whatever it contained was either very fragile or very precious.

He bowed – rather clumsily, hampered by whatever it was he held. Zaronel extended her hand to him, as she had done to his brother. This time, it trembled slightly. He took it and touched it briefly to his lips. 'You are welcome here, Princess Zaronel,' he said gruffly. 'I bring you a gift. I hope it pleases you.'

He set the bundle gently onto the floor, and carefully unwrapped it. There was a sudden scramble – a snuffle and a snort – the scrabble of tiny hooves. Zaronel's eyes flew wide with delighted disbelief. There on the scarlet carpet a tiny creature was struggling to its feet. Was it a pig? It could not have been more than a few hours old. It was covered in fine, silky hair, with a corkscrew tail at one end and a flat, questing snout at the other. Great ears like sails . . . bright, beady eyes . . . a head so covered in comical lumps and bumps that it was impossible to say whether it was the ugliest or the most beautiful creature she had ever seen.

'I found him in the forest,' Prince Zane was saying, 'lost and alone. He needs someone to look after him . . . and I thought . . .' He met her eyes, and in that moment she felt he could see straight into her soul. 'I thought you might be glad of a friend.'

Dawn of the second day. With the help of her handmaiden, Princess Zaronel arrayed herself in the shimmering gown symbolising the silver moon of Karazan, the silver in the twisted crown.

Karris braided silken threads of silver into Zaronel's hair as she sat silent at the window, gazing out into the drifting snow. Behind her the little piglet snored softly on the floor.

Again Princess Zaronel took her place in the throne room; again the trumpets sang and a figure appeared in the *distant doorway. She felt her heart give the tiniest skip; but then Prince Zeel was striding towards her over the red carpet, a dark-cloaked servant limping behind him.*

Zeel mounted the second step. Zaronel could smell the oil slicked into his hair; it had a cloying, sickly odour that caught in her throat.

His eyes slid slowly over her. When he spoke his whisper was too soft for any but her to hear. 'You are very beautiful, Princess Zaronel: a fitting jewel to adorn the crown of a king. The gift I bring you today is fair indeed, yet beside your loveliness it pales to nothing.'

The servant stepped forward. He carried a cushion covered with a cloth of rich brocade. With a flourish, Prince Zeel flicked the covering away and let it fall to the floor.

A ripple ran through the hall. On the cushion rested a gem of breathtaking beauty. It was a perfect sphere the size of a walnut, silver-grey in colour, its surface sheen deepening to a lustrous inner glow as if a dark light burned at its core.

Prince Zeel half-turned, his voice ringing through the great hall. 'Princess Zaronel of Antarion, on this the second day I bring you the Black Pearl of Karazeel: the name I shall take when I am king. At my command divers have scoured the oyster beds in its quest these two moons past, many perishing in the icy waters and treacherous currents of the southern seas. But at last the black oyster has been found, and the dark heart ripped from the flesh that has nurtured it for more than a hundred spans. This is my gift to you.'

The courtiers stirred and murmured. Zaronel's mouth

felt dry. She forced herself to speak, afraid her voice would catch in her throat, but her words came clearly, with only the slightest tremble. 'I thank you, Prince Zeel.'

Zeel stepped aside. There was a long, expectant hush. The two lines of trumpeters stood motionless, only their eyes moving as they awaited the signal to begin.

Zaronel felt a pulse beating at her throat, bringing a flush of hot blood to her cheeks.

The silence stretched on . . . and on.

And still he did not come.

Zaronel lay cold and still under her furs, pale moonlight spilling through the casement onto the bed. The little piglet lay at her feet. He was dreaming: she could feel the twitching of his tiny hooves and hear his snuffling grunts. Yesterday, the sound would have made her laugh aloud. Now, a single tear crept from under her dark lashes.

Then suddenly she heard music. The haunting song of a larigot, drifting through the open window.

Her heart leapt in her breast. She sprang up, her face flaming as she ran to the window and leaned out. Below, the golden stallion stamped and blew steam into the icy air. Prince Zane smiled up at her, the last notes of his serenade dying away in the darkness.

'I have a mind for a night ride,' he called softly. 'Would you come with me?'

Zaronel did not hesitate. She threw her shawl over her shoulders and snatched up a woollen cloak as she ran to the door. Eased it open . . . and came face to face with Zagros, wearing a scowl like thunder, his sword half-drawn.

Zaronel stared at him, heart hammering. She had forgotten that he would be on guard outside her door, as he was every night. He growled her name: the familiar nickname he had called her by since childhood. 'What is it? What has frightened you?'

'I – nothing, Zagros,' she replied haughtily. 'Put up your sword; nothing can harm me here! I . . . I could not sleep. I thought I might walk . . .'

He sheathed his sword. His mouth was a hard line, and his eyes bored into her. 'I will walk with you.'

'No! That is . . . I wish to walk alone.'

'Then you will not walk at all, Zaronel. Pray go back into your chamber.'

A flood of emotions swept through her. Anger, frustration . . . and a strange pull more powerful than any of them.

Beside Zagros, she seemed tiny; but she drew herself up and looked him full in the eye, every inch a princess. 'I go to ride with Prince Zane,' she said quietly. 'He awaits me at the foot of the tower.'

Zagros' mouth dropped open. 'What? You wish to ride out with the prince at night? Alone? Zaronel, surely even you can see –'

Her eyes flashed. 'I did not say I wish to ride; I said I go to ride. Do not stand in my way, Zagros. Remember who commands you.'

His face darkened with anger and wounded pride. There was something else, deep in his eyes – a twist of pain, as if a sword had been stabbed into his heart. She saw it, and knew it for what it was. 'Zagros,' she said gently, 'my safety alone is your concern, and I will be safe with him.

Do not hope for that which can never be. Stand aside now, and let me go.'

Silently, he stepped back and allowed her to pass. Stood like a statue with a heart of stone, hearing the quickening drum of hoof beats vanish into the night.

Prince Zane pulled the winged stallion to a halt on the crest of a low hill. Zaronel's cheeks were burning with cold, her hair a wild tangle from the ride. She could feel the raw energy of the horse under them, coiled like a spring to run again. She nestled safe as a child on the saddle in front of Prince Zane, his arms circling her, his solid warmth shielding her from the wind that swept the hillside. One gloved hand was steady on the reins, holding back the prancing stallion; the other drew his rough cloak round her shoulders. 'Zaronel.' The vibration of his voice on her bare neck made her shiver. 'Are you cold?'

'No,' she whispered. 'Not cold.'

'Here is my gift to you,' he said. 'Look up, Princess Zaronel. It is in the night sky.'

Obediently, she tilted her face upwards. Close – so close – wheeled a million stars. With his strong arms holding her, his breath warm on her hair, she felt they were the still point at the axis of the world, all the constellations of the universe spinning round them.

'Look.' He pointed. Above the horizon was a star like none she had ever seen before, bright with a light neither silver nor gold. She saw that it was moving, tracing a slow arc across the night sky; and as it moved it shed its radiance in a trail of iridescent stardust.

'The star is not mine to give,' he said, 'but it shall be known from this night forth as the Star of Zaronel. A star such as this carries a wish more powerful than any other. That wish is my gift to you.'

Zaronel closed her eyes and allowed her head to tilt back so that it rested against his chest. In the long silence that followed, under the light of the countless stars, she wished.

On the third day Princess Zaronel's handmaiden brought a gown of gold, with a golden veil like sunlight shining through rain to cover her face.

'I will dress myself today,' she said gently, taking the clothes from the handmaiden. She washed and readied herself as if in a trance, and brushed her hair into a shimmering cascade. Standing before the oval looking glass, she gazed long at her reflection, her grey eyes wide and full of dreams. At last she drew the veil over her face, and went out into the hallway where Zagros was waiting.

A tall man in robes the colour of mist stood beside the throne. He was neither young nor old; dark hair streaked with grey fell about his shoulders, and the inner dimension of the seer shadowed his eyes.

He spoke in a deep, clear voice that carried easily to the far end of the great hall, yet Zaronel felt his words were for her ears alone.

'I am Meirion, Prophet Mage of Karazan. The Symbols of Sovereignty are in my keeping. Today is the Third Day, the final day, the day on which gifts are given but not received.

184

'Only the gift of the winner of the Contest of Kings will be delivered into the hands of Princess Zaronel.

'And on this the Third Day, the nature of that contest will be made known.'

The trumpets rang out.

Prince Zeel strode down the red carpet, empty-handed and alone. He mounted the third step and stood before the princess. She felt the force of his will and quailed before it; sensed an emptiness deep within him, and an insatiable hunger for possession and power.

His lips barely moving, he spoke four words: 'You will be mine.'

He drew his sword with a hiss of steel and laid it on the step at Zaronel's feet. 'On this the third day I offer you my final gift. My sword has drunk deep of blood, yet its thirst is never sated. It is Blood-spiller, Widow-maker, Sorrow-bringer. I offer it to you and to the service of Antarion.'

Zaronel stared down at the sword. Its hilt was intricately wrought of dark metal, set with black gems. Even the blade was black.

She said nothing.

Again, the trumpets sang. As Prince Zane moved swiftly down the aisle towards her, Princess Zaronel felt she was drawing him to her with a silken cord wound tightly round her heart.

He reached her and knelt before her. If she had reached out, she could have touched him; run her hands through the tangle of his red-gold hair. She clasped her hands and waited.

He took a single scarlet rose from the folds of his cloak

and laid it at her feet. When he spoke, it was as if the two of them were alone in the great hall.

'I offer you my heart . . . my love . . . my life.'

Zaronel gazed down at the black sword and the red rose. Even when the silence was broken by the deep voice of Meirion, she did not lift her eyes.

'The Contest of Kings will take place on the morrow, at sunrise. It will be a race on horseback. The course will run from the eastern gate of Arakesh to the southern border of Shadowwood. A lone tree grows there with four golden leaves upon its branches. The princes will ride out, pluck one leaf, and return to Arakesh. Ride out again, and return with the second. The prince whose horse is last across the finish line will win the Twisted Crown of Karazan, the hand of Princess Zaronel, and the steward-ship of Antarion.'

There was a moment's silence, then a buzz that ran through the throne room like a swarm of bees.

Zeel stepped forward abruptly. 'But Mage Meirion,' he began, 'how can . . . do you not mean –'

'The prince whose horse is last will be the winner of the race. Last will be first, first last.' Meirion's face was expressionless.

'The Oracle has spoken. Tomorrow, at dawn.'

A BUNDLE OF RAGS

We woke before sunrise, stiff and cold. Jamie had insisted on taking the last watch; now he was snoring away on one corner of the tarpaulin we'd spread over our gear to protect it from chatterbot raids. The fire was out, but Rich's plan of weighting the tarp on every side with sleeping bodies had worked: our stuff was safe.

I'd expected to fall into a deep sleep the moment my head touched the ground. But for me the night had been full of dreams – unsettling, disjointed fragments that lingered long after I woke. I'd dreamed there were chatterbots close by in the forest, jibbering and calling . . . creeping still closer in the dark, busy fingers scrabbling at my sleeping bag. Then, in one of those dreamlike transformations, the fur-fringed faces of the chatterbots had changed to hooded heads looming over me, brushing my sleeping face with the chill of the grave . . . I'd jolted awake, heart hammering.

It had been the dawn breeze on my skin that had woken me. Now, tired and grumpy, I followed the others to the edge of the forest to look for twigs. The awkwardness of the previous day had evaporated overnight; as we fossicked between the scattered trees, the others' good-natured grousing and cheerful chatter drifted on the morning air.

'Would've been too bad if you'd escaped from the quicksand and then been hugged to death by the girls, huh, Jamie – though at least then the fire wouldn't have gone out . . .'

'*Richard!*'

'OK, Kenta, OK . . . hey, what d'you guys reckon about that diary? Old Zane strikes me as a bit of a cheapskate – Zeel's presents were way better, I'd say . . .'

A storm of protest greeted Rich's loudly voiced opinion. 'Your problem is that you don't have a romantic bone in your body – or if you have, it's covered in fat!' retorted Gen.

'Muscle, you mean . . .'

'I've been trying to figure out that horse race,' said Jamie thoughtfully. 'But Zeel was right for once – it just doesn't make sense.'

'So what else is new?' grumbled Rich.

'*First will be last, and last first* . . . typical Karazan,' said Gen.

'Perhaps that's the point: it's a puzzle, and they have to figure it out – just like we always do,' suggested Kenta.

'Hmmm. Like, get the horses to run backwards, or something? Would horses do that?'

'It's easy enough to come last in a race – *I* know that,' said Jamie ruefully. 'But not if everyone else is trying to as well.'

Suddenly the idle chatter was interrupted by a sharp cry: a wordless exclamation of shock and revulsion.

It was Gen. She was almost invisible among the shadows of the trees, crouched over something on the ground. Rich gave me a grin and a wink as we hurried across. 'Probably a worm. You know Gen . . .'

Gen had backed off, face crumpling as if she was about to cry. Cautiously, I followed Rich closer. It was easy to see what had brought Gen over there: the ground all round was strewn with dry sticks that would make perfect kindling. She was staring, pointing at a fallen tree trunk, rotting and covered in mossy lichen . . . and suddenly I knew it wasn't a worm. The nagging feeling of unease I'd had since waking was stronger; I felt the back of my neck prickle, and the hairs on my arms rise. 'Hold on, Rich – be careful . . .'

Then we saw it. Half-hidden behind the tree trunk: a filthy, rumpled bundle of rags.

Kenta was behind me, peering warily over my shoulder. Rich gave us all a sheepish grin, and I realised he'd been worried for a moment too. 'Come on, Gen – toughen up! It's someone's old socks or something, that's all.'

But it was too big to be socks. A cloak, maybe . . . or a pack, discarded for some reason.

Rich bent and picked up a long stick. Old socks

or not, he wasn't about to touch it till he was sure, I noticed. Sidling forward, he brought the stick closer, ready to give the dark shape an exploratory poke.

A sudden squawk from Kenta made us jump. 'Don't, Richard! Leave it! It's . . . oh, it's . . .'

I caught her arm to stop her dashing forward. 'It's what? Don't touch it, Kenta: you never know –'

She jerked away, and before I could stop her she was over on her knees beside the log, reaching over with both hands. '*Kenta* . . .' Rich might as well have saved his breath.

'Oh!' The softest exclamation, trembling on the edge of tears. 'It's a chatterbot! A poor little dead chatterbot.'

'Ugh!' said Jamie. 'Adam's right – don't touch it. It's probably full of maggots.'

'No, it's still warm – feel!' Kenta lifted the limp, filthy body of the chatterbot out from behind the log, holding it out for us to see with her eyes full of tears.

'Aw, c'mon, Kenta,' grumbled Rich awkwardly, 'there's nothing to cry about. It's nature's way, you know? Survival of the fittest. Ask Jamie – he'll tell you. Must happen all the time here in Chattering Wood.'

'It's just . . .' she gulped, staring down at the small, limp body, 'it's just that it reminds me so much of Blue-bum.'

There was a long, awful silence. We all stared at the dead chatterbot in Kenta's arms.

190

It was Jamie who said it. 'That's because it *is* Blue-bum. I'd know him anywhere. It's our Blue-bum. Something terrible has happened to him, and he's dead.'

BLUE-BUM

I stared down at the small, still body. I couldn't
believe it – wouldn't. One chatterbot looked
much the same as another – there were hordes of
them in the forest, transformed from whatever they'd
been before by drinking water from the talking stream.
Who drinks of me shall be a chatterbot . . .

This could be any one of them . . . surely?

But I was in denial, and I knew it.

He lay in Kenta's arms like an old, discarded toy.
His fur, once so soft and silky, was tangled and matted
with grime and what looked like dried blood. His
face was oddly shrivelled, as if death had somehow
folded it in on itself.

Rich was talking, his voice seeming to come from
very far away. '. . . so if this really *is* Blue-bum – and
I'm not convinced – then he was here in Chattering
Wood, not selling us down the river to Karazeel like
we thought.'

'And that'd mean it wasn't Weevil who helped him
with the computer program,' said Gen slowly.

'But then who was it?' objected Jamie. 'They could

192

never have figured it out themselves – not in a million years!'

'I told you he'd never have done it!' cried Kenta fiercely. 'Poor thing – he must have tried to join the other chatterbots and been driven out, attacked . . .' Her voice caught, and a tear plopped into the caked fur round the puckered little face.

'Unless . . .' said Richard.

'Unless what?' Kenta glared at him.

'Unless he *did* help them – for whatever reason. I know you never really trusted him, Adam. And once they were finished with him, they threw him out . . . and he came here.'

'He wouldn't have helped them! Maybe at first, when he was Weevil still . . . but he changed. You know he did!' Kenta was sobbing now. 'He gave up his chance of escaping so we could get away – or have you forgotten that?'

'Wait a second.' There was an odd expression on Gen's face. 'Look at him – *really* look. Look at the state he's in . . . and think about what it means. Yes, he's obviously been attacked – killed – by the other chatterbots. But there are things . . .' she hesitated, 'things the chatterbots couldn't have done. Look at his hands.'

I looked. The blood drained from my face. Blue-bum's hands were curled into loose fists, but I could clearly see that what had once been blunt-fingered, nimble monkey-paws had been grotesquely stretched and twisted. The fingers were cruelly deformed, the

193

nails crooked-looking as if someone had tried to wrench them out.

'He's been tortured,' said Jamie blankly. 'Horribly tortured, to make him tell.'

'Look at his fur,' whispered Gen. 'There are patches missing everywhere, where it's been yanked out.' It was true – Blue-bum's once-glossy fur had a mangy, balding look. 'And his face. Even now, you can see the pain.' She was right. It was no wonder we hadn't recognised him at first. The leathery little face had a pathetic, shrunken look, etched with lines that made him look as if he'd aged a hundred years.

'It doesn't matter, anyhow,' said Kenta. 'Whatever he did or didn't do – whatever the reasons – it's over.'

'What now?' asked Richard bleakly.

I swallowed. Someone had to say it. But still, I could hardly get the words out. 'We'll bury him. It's the last thing we can do for him; the only thing.'

I gazed down at him one last time. It was Blue-bum, and yet it wasn't. *That's what death does, I guess.*

A fat tear rolled down Kenta's cheek and fell onto his face; then another.

And his skin gave the tiniest twitch.

Blue-bum was swaddled in Kenta's cloak by the fire, only his face peeking out. His mouth was open a chink, and when I put my hand right up to it I could feel the faintest whisper of breath. His eyes were still closed. He wasn't dead – yet. But I reckoned he was about as close to it as it was possible to get.

Where there was life . . .

'Rich – the healing potion! It's in my bag, wrapped in my shawl – quick!' There wasn't much left, but it would be more than enough to save a little chatterbot.

Kenta eased the cloak back from the little face and held him upright. I could feel the others crowded behind me. Carefully, I tipped a smidgen out of the shimmering crystal phial; there were still a few drops left, if we needed them. Held out the spoon, the potion gleaming in its silver bowl like a liquid pearl. 'OK, Kenta, here we go . . .'

As I spoke, Blue-bum's eyelids flickered and his eyes opened the minutest crack. They were dull and clouded, moving sluggishly from face to face as if he didn't recognise us.

Kenta bent close, whispering urgently. 'Blue-bum – Weevil – it's us – Kenta and Gen and the boys! Oh, Blue-bum, what have they done to you? Don't give up – please! Look: we've got the healing potion. One tiny sip and you'll be well again.'

As we watched, the blankness in the button eyes was focusing into consciousness . . . recognition. If we needed any further proof that this was really Blue-bum, it was here, in the beginnings of a slit smile, weak as it was. But then suddenly his face contorted. Instead of opening his mouth like I'd expected, he shut it tight as a trap . . . turned his face away and squeezed his eyes closed, as if he wanted to blot out not only our faces, but the entire world.

'Whatever's the matter? Don't you understand – it's

your only hope! Just a little, please, for me . . .' begged Kenta.

My mind was spinning in circles. Blue-bum knew about the potion – knew its power. In his place, I'd have been swigging down every drop I could lay my hands on. He must surely know how close to death he was – so why . . .

'*Do you want to die?*' Kenta wailed.

Suddenly Gen was kneeling next to her, reaching out gentle hands to Blue-bum for the first time. 'You poor little thing! That's it – don't you see?' She looked up at us, tears shining on her cheeks. 'That's exactly what he wants! He feels he's betrayed us all. Oh, Blue-bum . . . we've seen your poor hands; we know what they did to you. You couldn't help it. No one blames you. We couldn't bear it if you died. Take the potion – please – for all our sakes . . .'

Very, very slowly, Blue-bum's head turned back. His eyes squinched reluctantly open, creeping hesitantly from face to face as if he was afraid of what he might see there. Anxious, eager faces peered back at him.

He looked at me last of all: a pitiful look that said clearer than words: *And you, Adam? How about you? Can you find it in your heart to forgive me . . . for everything?*

I gazed back at him, deep into his eyes. Something was niggling at the back of my mind, but I pushed it aside; forced myself to smile. 'Come on, Blue-bum:

drink up like a good boy,' I said gruffly. 'Whatever's happened in the past can stay there. We don't hold it against you – not a single one of us.'

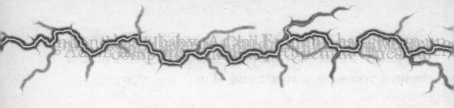

POOR LITTLE GUY

If we'd expected the potion to transform Blue-
bum back into his old self, we were disappointed.
Within a few moments he was sitting up, looking
round alertly, and tucking into the plateful of tempt-
ing morsels the girls prepared for him like a chatterbot
who hasn't seen food for a year. Any obvious injuries
there might have been – cuts, bites and abrasions –
had healed without a trace, but it took over an hour
with a facecloth and soap, Kenta's water canteen and
a comb to clean him up.

But whatever had been done to him seemed to go
too deep for even the magical potion to cure completely. Apart from his scrawny body, moth-eaten fur
and crippled hands, there was something in his eyes
that hadn't been there before – or not for a long while,
anyhow. The bright, inquisitive gaze had gone. In its
place was a wary watchfulness, like a stray dog wondering where the next kick is coming from. Saddest of
all, while he used to move easily, cantering along with
long, loping strides and shimmying up and down trees
like a spider monkey, now he could barely hobble.

Rich and I sat silently, bags packed and ready to go, watching Jamie and the girls fuss over him. At least, Kenta and Gen were fussing; it turned out Jamie had a more serious agenda. 'By the way, Blue-bum,' he said oh-so-casually, teasing the last few tangles out of the fur on Weevil's tail, 'those guys Karazeel and Evor: what exactly are they planning, d'you know? And more important, when? 'Cos it'd really help us if we knew, and it'd kind of make up for what you –'

A jibbering chitter interrupted him. At the sound of Karazeel and Evor's names, Blue-bum had flinched as if he'd been hit; now he was cringing away, scooting backwards on his blue buttocks till only Jamie's hold on his tail stopped him going further. Jamie saw us all watching and let go, blushing beetroot-red. 'Sorry,' he mumbled. 'I just . . .'

Kenta scowled at him. 'Well, don't. Poor Blue-bum's gone through more than we can ever imagine. It isn't fair to expect him to re-live any part of it.'

Blue-bum limped across to her and scrambled clumsily onto her lap. She gave him a defensive hug, still glaring at Jamie. Rich and I exchanged a glance. Truth was, I'd had the exact same idea as Jamie, though I'd planned to give Blue-bum a bit longer to settle in before debriefing him; and by the look on Rich's face, he had too. But now Jamie had blown it – if there'd ever been anything to blow. Blue-bum could chatter and chitter and jabber and gibber and do everything except actually talk, so the most we'd ever be able to hope for would be a kind of twenty questions, with yes/no answers.

And now, not even that.

In the end it was almost lunchtime before we finally got going. Kenta, in her self-appointed role of head nurse, made a nest in her pack with her cloak; Bluebum snuggled down comfortably in it with his head peeking out, watching the rest of us share out her gear with what I thought was a rather smug expression.

'We need to make up for lost time,' growled Rich as we shouldered our now much-heavier packs. I nodded agreement. There was an edgy, anxious flutter under my ribs – the same pressured, scooped-out feeling you have when you know you're going to be really late for school.

'Oh, stop being so grumpy,' said Gen, with an irritating toss of her tawny head. 'Typical male: can't bear to see anyone else get any attention. Come on, Kenta, we'll lead the way – and if you boys can keep up, I'll be impressed!'

Sure enough, she and Kenta raced off at a pace I was prepared to bet would burn them out in an hour. Jamie trundled along behind them, the occasional 'Wait up, girls!' drifting back to Rich and me.

It wasn't long before we'd left the forest far behind and begun the slow ascent into the mountains. The track, which we'd joined up with north of Chattering Wood, began to wind and zigzag as it climbed. Far ahead we could see the dark dots of Jamie and the girls toiling upwards.

Last time we'd done this climb it had been autumn, in mist so thick we could barely see the path. Now, blazing sun beat down on our backs; I could feel my neck beginning to burn, and my shirt sticking to my back under my pack.

Behind me I could hear Rich huffing and puffing; ahead rose fold upon fold of nubbly grey-green hillside, steepening to rocky crags on the horizon. I stopped to wait for Rich, panting, pretending to admire the view.

The mountains stretched away on both sides, tumbling down in the east to purple plains patched with forest, and the occasional flash of distant sea. On the other side ran the main mountain range, north-south, dwarfing the one we were struggling up. The afternoon sun was lowering to meet its jagged peaks, the angle of its rays making the looming slopes seem semi-transparent, as insubstantial as gauze.

Rich came up beside me, wiping his forehead on his sleeve. 'The track seems rougher than last time,' he said when he'd regained his breath; 'or is it just me?'

I looked back the way we'd come, considering. It did seem more eroded. Slips were making the going treacherous here and there, even on these lower slopes; there was more slippery scree than I remembered, and the path was overgrown in places with brush and grass.

There was another difference too. Last time I'd had this constant electric tingle at the back of my neck; a feeling that at any moment someone was about to come up the track behind us. And with good reason: the track was the main thoroughfare between Arakesh and Shakesh, King Karazeel's stronghold. Now, that tingling feeling was gone. Looking back as far as I could see, right back to the distant smudge of Chattering Wood, there was only emptiness. And I felt in my bones it would stay that way.

I shrugged, and shot Richard a weary grin. 'Maybe. Or it could just be that it's so hot. I don't think there's such a thing as perfect weather for climbing a mountain, do you?'

We set off again, Rich in the lead now, me plugging along behind. There was something else on my mind: a thought I couldn't shake, weighing heavier by far than the pack on my back.

'Rich . . .' I said hesitantly, 'how does old Weevil – Blue-bum, I mean – seem, to you?'

'What d'you mean, how does he seem?' Rich grunted. 'Seems like he's had a tough time, poor little guy. But he'll come right. Bound to, all the TLC he's getting.'

We trudged on. Then: 'Why? How does he seem to you?'

I didn't want to say it. *Different*. We *knew* he was different; it was painfully, pitifully obvious. And I knew exactly what Richard would say if I tried to explain the slightly sick, lead-weight feeling in my gut. 'Better not let Kenta hear you say that,' he'd say. And, 'Let's face it, Adam, you never liked him. Poor little guy.'

But that wasn't true. I had liked him, once he'd sprouted a tail and a bright blue bum; once he'd stopped stalking me, and turned cool and funny and sparky. Now that bright spirit was broken, at least for the time being, and through no fault of his. So what was my problem? Was I really the kind of guy who couldn't forgive someone for doing exactly what I'd have done myself, in the same position?

I kicked at a stone and watched it bound away down the mountainside, bouncing and spinning till it disappeared into nothingness.

I realised Rich was still waiting for an answer.

'Yeah,' I muttered, 'seems like he has had it pretty tough. Poor little guy.'

THE EMPTY COWL

It wasn't long before Rich and I caught up with Jamie and the girls. We were together when at last, towards evening, we struggled over the millionth false summit and found nothing above us except pale eggshell sky.

Ahead of us the track levelled out, winding across a broad saddle of flat ground before diving between two scree-covered slopes and plunging out of sight: Draken Pass. To our left a scatter of low houses crouched in the deep shadow of the peaks which reared up on every side, a backdrop of dark conifers spilling down the mountainside behind it.

Drakendale.

A narrow path left the main track and led to the village.

'Well,' said Rich, 'here we are. What next?'

'I guess we find a friendly villager and strike up a conversation with him,' said Jamie without much conviction. 'Ask how the village got its name; stuff like that.'

'Problem is, I don't see any villagers, friendly or otherwise,' said Rich.

He was right: there wasn't a soul in sight . . . and there was something distinctly unwelcoming about the deserted-looking cluster of houses. Smoke twisted up from one or two chimneys, but other than that there was no sign of life. Now we were finally here, I realised with a sinking feeling that I had almost completely lost confidence in our reason for coming. Had we really come all this way because two lines in the poem seemed to suggest that Prince Zephyr was somehow hidden in the eyes of a dragon . . . and because the word *draken* had been mistaken for *dragon* by yours truly, never the world's greatest reader?

As we straggled closer, I saw there were lights shining from some of the windows – the dim flicker of candles or a cooking fire. Most of the buildings – and there were no more than a dozen or so – were grouped round what I supposed was the village green, if you could call it that: a rough open area of patchy brown grass and bare, stony earth. In its centre was a stunted tree bearing a few wizened leaves; beside it a rusty hand-pump dripped water into a stone trough.

Some of the buildings were obviously houses: squat rectangles with a low door flanked by grimy windows. As we passed the first one I felt a prickling certainty that we were being watched. I walked on, resisting the temptation to look behind me: past the open double doors of a forge, the flagstones drifting with grey ash, the anvil silent, the furnace cold . . . past a row of dilapidated stables in a deserted courtyard. Next to it was a ramshackle double-storey stone building with a sign hanging from a rusty wrought-iron bracket above the door. The sign was swaying slightly in the wind, making an eerie creaking vibration like old, arthritic bones, or the sound of a rusty seesaw far away: up and down; to and fro.

The Empty Cowl.

'What's a cowl?' asked Rich in a loud whisper.

'Shhhh!' hissed Gen.

'It's a hood, like a monk wears. Look at the picture,' breathed Jamie.

I looked. It was faded faint as a ghost . . . a grey hood, with only darkness where the face should be.

The Empty Cowl. A chill trickled down my spine. That was what I could feel – what all of us had felt the moment we'd left the main track. The whole place reeked of them: the Faceless. They weren't here now: if they had been, we would have known it long before. What I was sensing was the shadowy residue of their presence . . . a lingering body odour of evil.

'I don't like it here,' quavered Gen, glancing uneasily over her shoulder.

Looking round at the unhappy faces of the others, I could tell that no one did. But we'd come all this way, and now we were here . . .

'Come on, guys: think positive,' I said cheerfully. 'That sign means one of two things: this is either an up-market clothing boutique or an inn. And I know which my money's on.' I fished out one of the gold coins, spun it in the air and caught it. 'This time round, we're bucks-up. Who's for a hot meal that hasn't been cooked on a camp fire – and maybe even a real bed for the night? I say we go on in and see where it takes us.'

Reluctantly, the others agreed. We'd keep our eyes and ears wide open, say as little as we could possibly get away with, and – most important of all – double-check with the others before any of us made a single move.

'You can be our spokesman, Adam,' said Jamie, with a meaningful glance at Rich. 'You look the oldest – but more important, you talk the least.' It was ages since Rich got so carried away with his performance at the Brewer's Butt, but none of us had forgotten the consequences.

'Better make sure old Blue-bum's well hidden, Kenta,' countered Rich with a grin; 'they may not allow pets.' An indignant chitter from the depths of the pack made us all smile, even Gen. I pulled my hood well over my face, checked that the others had done the same . . . then took a deep breath, opened the door and walked in.

We were in a low-ceilinged, smoky room lit by a couple of overhead lanterns. A fire smouldered sullenly on the far wall. There were half a dozen tables on the stone-flagged floor, the one nearest the fire occupied by three rough-looking men with swarthy, bearded faces. A wooden counter ran the length of the wall closest to us, its surface cluttered with iron-hooped barrels I guessed must contain ale or wine, and an untidy array of tankards, goblets and dusty-looking bottles. A couple of men stood at the counter, and one – in a stained apron that might once have been white – behind it: the innkeeper.

As we walked into the room, absolute silence fell. Every head turned slowly to stare at us, on every face the same expression: wariness and hostility. I set my own face into grim, unfriendly lines to match. Instinct told me nothing would be gained by using Matron's best manners here, trotting up to the counter cap in hand like children begging a favour. Ignoring every-one, I slouched across to a vacant table near the window, shrugged off my backpack and settled down facing the room, gesturing the others onto the chairs beside me.

'Adam!' hissed Jamie, bug-eyed with disapproval. 'You can't just walk in – it's not polite! You should . . .'

'Should what?' I gave him my best Karazan glower. 'This is an inn, isn't it? Let him come to us.'

Sure enough, after a muttered exchange with his cronies the innkeeper sidled over, anything but welcoming. 'Well?' he snarled. 'What do *you* want?'

'Food – and beds for the night,' I growled back, snapping the coin down on the table with a loud *click*. I only hoped it would be enough. Automatically, the innkeeper's eyes followed the sound, narrowing suspiciously . . . then widened to a look of almost comical astonishment. His mouth dropped open.

A sly, greedy expression crept over his face. 'It is many spans since we have seen an old gold crown in these parts . . . especially in the hands of one so young. How came you by it?'

Here we go, I thought: *question time. But one thing's for sure – the money* is *enough. More than.* The listening silence in the room – along with common sense – told me that the fewer questions we answered, the better. I met his eyes levelly. 'Food and a room,' I said.

For a long moment his eyes stared back into mine, cunning and calculating; then dropped to the coin. It lay between us on the rough, fissured surface of the table, seeming to glow with its own golden light, the strong profile of the king gazing fearlessly at infinity. Suddenly, I wished I didn't have to part with it. I desperately wanted to keep it – more than I wanted hot food, more than I longed for a comfortable bed and a good night's sleep.

Most of all, I wanted to find out the truth: to discover what had become of Zane and Zaronel; to find Zephyr, not only to save our own world, but to put right whatever wrongs had been done to them, and to all of Karazan.

'Ask for something to drink, Adam,' Jamie was hissing under his breath. 'Something hot . . . cocoa, maybe . . .'

I looked round at the faces of my friends: tired and dirty, tension and fear giving way to a kind of weary hope. I pushed the coin across to the innkeeper. 'And something hot to drink.'

It wasn't long before a frowzy woman with frizzy hair came waddling through from the kitchen with a laden tray. Two trips later the table was groaning: a cottage loaf of dark, crusty bread; a whole cheese, amber-coloured, crumbly and sharp-smelling; five steaming bowls of stew, fragrant gravy thick with vegetables and tender meat falling off the bone.

The final trip brought our 'cocoa': steaming pewter goblets full to the brim with something the colour of rubies. The steam curled up my nose and straight into my bloodstream, strangely sweet and sour together; it tasted of hot grapes and spices, liquid velvet warming me to the tips of my toes.

'I could drink this all night,' said Jamie cheerily a short while later, draining his glass and burping.

'Might be better if you didn't,' I told him, giving Rich a wink. 'And now, if we've finished, I think we should find our room and get some sleep.' I had a hunch our host might happen to pass our table soon, and stop for a chat – he'd find more than one tongue loosened by whatever had been in those goblets.

Sure enough, he was heading across the room, wiping down tables, working his way steadily nearer.

I shook off my feeling of woozy wellbeing, levered myself up and intercepted him. 'I think you have forgotten something,' I said quietly.

'Forgotten something?' he blustered. 'I know not what you mean –'

'I think you do,' I said evenly, holding out my hand.

'Oh. Why yes, of course . . .'

He bustled over to the counter, and made a great show of fumbling beneath it. Eventually he produced a worn-looking drawstring bag and counted out a number of coins, tipping them into my outstretched hand.

They could have been gold and silver tiddlywinks for all I knew, but I frowned intently down at them, pretending to check them carefully before slipping them into my pocket. There were plenty of them. Even if he was cheating us – which I didn't doubt he'd do if he could get away with it, helped along by the hot toddy – I wouldn't need to break into our remaining crown too soon.

At that moment the door creaked open behind me, icy wind gusting down my neck. I wheeled round, all the fears that had been banished by warmth and food returning with a rush. But it was just an old man coming in for a jug of something to keep out the cold; he shuffled through the door, pulling it closed behind him. I headed back to our table to try to dislodge the others, half-watching him out of the corner of my eye. There was something about him . . .

Back at the table, Kenta was talking to the others in an urgent undertone. 'It *is*, I tell you! I'd know him anywhere!' Everyone was staring first at her, then across the room at the old man, who had settled on a bench beside the fire and was slowly unwinding the heavy woollen scarf that swathed his face. Even

Blue-bum was peeping out of Kenta's pack, eyes bright and inquisitive, a half-nibbled piece of cheese held awkwardly in one crooked paw.

'Don't you remember? *Drakendale!*' Kenta's eyes were glowing with excitement, her cheeks flushed.

Rich shifted uneasily. 'Relax, Kenta,' he said in a voice he obviously hoped was soothing. 'One old man looks pretty much like the next, especially all wrapped up like a Christmas pudding. And it was ages ago . . .'

'Don't patronise me, Richard!' she snapped, suddenly sounding just like Gen. 'I know when I'm right! And I'm going to, so there!'

I drew breath to ask, 'Going to what?' But it was too late.

Open-mouthed, I watched – we all watched – as Kenta marched across the room and plonked herself down onto the bench beside the old man, chattering away nineteen to the dozen and smiling up into his scowling hatchet face as if he was her long-lost grandfather.

ASHLING

'So much for no one making a move without the others' say-so,' grumbled Rich.

Things were moving way too fast for me. Whatever made Kenta think she recognised the old guy? It wasn't as if we had a vast network of acquaintances in Karazan; as far as I knew, we'd only ever met one old man before: Meirion. And it certainly wasn't him.

'I don't get it,' I said. 'Who does Kenta think –'

'She can tell you herself,' said Richard grimly. 'Here she comes.'

Over by the fire, the old guy was on his feet again, the scarf dangling from his hand, apparently forgotten. He was staring across at us with an odd expression on his face. At the bar, the innkeeper and his friends were watching with undisguised interest.

Kenta was dodging between the tables, gabbling away before she even reached us. 'It *is* him! I knew it! Danon of Drakendale: that's his name! Adam, *you* remember him – the poor man with the sick daughter.'

How could I have forgotten? An old man struggling

213

down the aisle of the Sacred Temple of Arakesh
wheeling a rickety barrow . . . falling to his knees to
beg the Curator of Healing for the magical potion that
would save his daughter's life . . . the huddled form
under the threadbare blanket, so small and still. His
words, trembling with desperation: *We have begged
gelden from kin both far and near . . . sold all we have
save the roof over our heads to raise the price for the potion
that will heal her.* But it hadn't been enough. He was
sent away empty-handed.

'. . . her name is Ashling and she's still alive – *a
living death* – I've told him we can help – come *on*!'

'But Kenta –' Jamie began.

'But what?' Her dark eyes sparked. 'James
Fitzpatrick, are you telling me you have a problem
with giving Ashling the last of our healing potion?'

Jamie flushed and looked down, shuffling his feet.
'Well, not exactly. It's just . . .'

'Just?'

'Just that . . . well, Karazan's real dangerous. And
. . . we might need it ourselves.'

'Jamie's right, Kenta,' said Richard in a low voice.
'You need to calm down and think logically. I'm real
sorry for the old dude – we all are. But it's not our
problem. We gave the potion to Blue-bum, because
. . . well, because he's one of us. But we can't go dishing it out to every Tom, Dick and Harry we happen to
bump into. Jamie's right: what if we need it ourselves,
and it's all gone?'

Kenta sank down onto her chair as if in slow

motion. She stared from Rich to Jamie and back again. 'I can't believe I'm hearing this.'

'Neither can I,' chipped in Gen in a furious whisper. 'You boys are so selfish! Don't you remember how we felt when we saw that poor man wheeling his barrow out of the Temple, the tears streaming down his face? I'd have done anything to help him – I thought we all would. And now, when we have the chance – I can't *believe* it!'

'Calm down, Gen,' soothed Rich, looking warily at Gen's clenched fists. 'I'm not saying –'

'Will you *stop* telling us to calm down?' hissed Gen. 'And if you're not saying that, what *are* you saying?'

'Just that we should think it through,' mumbled Rich miserably.

'And you didn't have any right to promise him the potion without consulting us first, Kenta,' said Jamie righteously. 'Who's going to tell him he can't have it after all, just when his hopes are up?'

We all looked over at Danon. He was standing with his shoulders bowed, eyes fixed on the floor, the tattered old scarf twisted between his hands. He was obviously trying not to listen to our conversation, but by the look on his face he'd heard every word.

'I say we put it to the vote,' said Jamie at last, sounding very subdued. 'But we need to remember that this is about . . .' he dropped his voice even lower, '. . . about far more than the life of one child, as important as that is. We're on a mission – we all know what – and we need every bit of help we can get. I'm really, really sorry, Kenta, but I vote we keep what's left of the potion for ourselves – just in case.'

'Me too,' said Rich gruffly.

'I'm with you, Kenta,' said Gen, giving Kenta's hand a squeeze. 'So, Adam: looks like you have the casting vote.'

I stared down at the table. What the boys said was true. If one of us had an accident – like Jamie had – and the potion was finished . . . what then? My head told me that with so much at stake we'd be fools to give something so precious away.

But then Q's words drifted back into my mind: the advice he'd given us so long ago, way back at Quested Court before we'd set off on our first adventure to Karazan. *Much may occur with a hidden purpose that will only become apparent later . . .*

My head told me to vote with the boys; my heart told me differently.

I raised my head slowly, drawing a breath to say something, though I hadn't yet decided what.

He was gone.

Without thinking I was on my feet and crossing to the door, dimly aware of the others scraping back their chairs to follow me. I flung the door open and stumbled out into the darkness, gazing wildly round. Deep night had fallen; a thin sliver of moon glimmered through distant treetops; the sky jangled with stars. The air crackled with cold; far away I could hear the lonely howl of the wind in the crags.

The old man was nowhere.

Then I saw it – a chink of light as he let himself quietly through the door of the very last house. A few strides and I was there, the rough wood under my knuckles as I rapped once, twice, then waited.

Behind me, a hand found mine and squeezed.

The door opened.

Ashling lay motionless on the truckle bed in the corner of the tiny room. Last time I'd seen her it had just been a fleeting impression of a dark, swaddled shape; now I could see she was a real little girl about Hannah's age. Her face would have been pretty if it hadn't had such a strange, frightening blankness; it was grey and lifeless, a smudge of ash under the tangle of dull black hair. She could have been sleeping, but her stillness was a million miles from sleep. Her body was here, but her spirit was far away.

'She has been thus since the day she first fell ill,' Danon whispered. 'Never waking, never moving. These many, many moons.'

The mother sat at the head of the bed, her eyes locked on the face of her daughter, her hands clasped in her lap. Her face was seamed with weariness, dull with pain, blurred by a terrible, helpless patience. Even when Danon told her why we had come her expression didn't change; she simply shook her head slowly from side to side, then reached out a gentle hand and smoothed the hair back from the child's brow. 'She hoped too long in vain,' Danon murmured; 'now she dares hope no longer.'

I touched the back of my fingers to the girl's pale cheek. It was cold as marble. *You must come back now. However distant you are, however long and hard the journey.*

I took out my shawl and unfolded it. The crystal phial gleamed in the soft candlelight. Holding it up, I could see the potion: liquid mother-of-pearl, glowing with the promise of life.

I knelt beside the mother and gently unclasped her hands. They felt dry and papery and very cold. I pressed the phial into her palm, curled the fingers round . . . felt the tingle of magic pass from my hand to hers.

Her eyes widened and focused, as if she was waking from a dream. She turned her head, slowly, slowly, and looked at me. I looked back, deep into her eyes; saw the first faint light of hope flicker there, then burn with a strong, steady brightness.

I stood, and looked down at them both for a moment. How many long days and nights had they spent like this, mother and child enclosed in their silent shell of candlelight? And now it was over.

I turned away and left them, gesturing to the others to follow me out into the night.

'So much for being good Samaritans,' grumbled Rich, stomping along beside me back to the inn. 'Not so much as a *thank you* – and we didn't even get to see if it worked!'

I didn't answer. For once I wasn't in the mood for Rich's bluster and bravado. What I really wanted was to be on my own. 'You go in,' I told the others as we reached the inn. 'I'll just . . .' The words caught in my throat.

'Shall I stay with you, Adam?' offered Jamie shyly. 'It's real dark and scary . . .'

I smiled and shook my head. A wedge of yellow light spilled briefly out into the night, and at last I was alone.

The moon had risen higher now, a shining crescent among the silvery stars. The wind had dropped, and the night was very still. I walked over to the wizened tree and leaned back against it, my cloak wrapped round me, gazing up at the sky.

As I watched, a dot of light bloomed in the blackness, painting a hair-fine brushstroke across the sky before fading away to nothing. Ashling's spirit, arcing through the heavens on its journey back to make her whole again? I smiled at myself; I'd been in Karazan too long. It was only a shooting star. I thought of the Star of Zaronel, and of Prince Zane's gift: *the most powerful wish of all . . .*

Long ago, on another moonlit night in Karazan, we'd talked about what each of us would choose if we were granted one wish. Everyone had their turn except me. Now I wondered: could I take this shooting-star wish for myself and use it – for real? And if I did, what would I wish for? I didn't know. Sometimes – like now – I had a strange ache deep inside, in my soul, almost: a kind of emptiness. I would wish for whatever it was that would heal that ache and make

219

me feel complete; but the problem was, I didn't have any idea what it could be.

I was still gazing at the place the star had disappeared when I heard the soft scrape of a footfall behind me.

I spun round, my heart in my throat. A dark, cloaked figure was moving towards me through the darkness. It was holding something in its hand . . .

'I am sorry if I startled you.' It was a second before I recognised the voice of the old man, Danon. He sounded different: stronger, surer. Happy. 'I saw you from the window. I wanted to tell you . . . she has awoken, and though she is very weak, she knew our faces and smiled. We can never repay you and your friends for what you have given us.'

'We were glad to.'

'No – let me go on. For all of us now – not only Ashling – there is a future. Drakendale has become a place of the dead. For too long it has been used as a way-station by . . . by those who travelled the north road to Shakesh. I am a carpenter: my calling is to craft things of beauty from wood, revealing the hidden inner form through the art of chisel and saw. Yet these many spans my skills have been harnessed to the service of King Karazeel, building and repairing wagons, yokes, carts . . . and cages.'

'And now?'

'Now they say the king's new stronghold is complete. This road is used no more, and we are free to go. Many of the townsfolk have already left, for a

220

shadow lies over Drakendale, darkening the hearts of those who remain. For us, with Ashling as she was . . . the journey would have been impossible. Now, in a few short days, she will be strong enough to leave.'

'Where will you go?'

'To Arakesh, or the port of Kaladar – who knows? But at last we are free. Here.' He pressed something into my hand. 'This gift is humble, but it is all we have to give.'

I looked down at it. It was a small bottle made of thick, dark-coloured glass, with a cork stopper. 'Thank you,' I mumbled. Even in the darkness, I could see his expression: a kind of shy pride, as if whatever he was giving me was far more precious than he pretended – at least to him. 'What is it?' I ventured.

'I call it my revealing oil. It will bring out the hidden grain in even the plainest timber. You will find it nowhere else in Karazan, for I make it myself, from the sap of a secret tree that grows deep in the mountain forests.'

'Well . . . that's . . .' I wasn't sure what to say. What use would this ever be to us? Still, as Hannah would have said, it's the thought that counts. I unstopped the cork and took an appreciative sniff. It smelled the way pine trees do after rain – a fresh, resinous, golden smell. 'Mmmm. That's really special. Thank you very much. We'll treasure it.'

'I only wish I could give you more. But now . . .' He turned to go.

'Wait, Danon . . . before you go. There is one thing.'

I couldn't believe I hadn't thought of it before. I hadn't consulted the others – but then I hadn't had the chance. 'I don't suppose ...' I was racking my brains for a way to make the question sound casual, the kind of throw-away line you'd come out with just because it happened to pop into your head. 'You don't happen to know of any ... uh ... *dragons* round here, do you? Not necessarily a *real* dragon,' I said, remembering Jamie's complicated theory; 'just something ... dragon-*like*? *D-d-draken*-like, maybe?' I could feel myself blushing scarlet.

Danon gave me a shrewd, searching look. For a moment I was sure he thought I'd gone totally crazy. But then he smiled, as if I'd answered a question he hadn't even asked. 'Ah,' he said. 'I confess I wondered why a party of travellers so young would be so far from home. So, you are off on an adventure: in search of the mythical dragon that gives the mountains their name!' He laughed: an odd, rusty sound, as if it hadn't been used for a long time. I saw he wasn't nearly as old as I'd thought; with laugh lines on his face, standing straight and tall, he seemed a different person from the pathetic figure of an hour ago. 'Why, how many times did I myself roam these mountains as a child, chasing the dreams conjured by firelight tales . . . but that was long ago.'

My heart gave a peculiar little skip. 'You were looking for it too! And did you ever find anything?' I asked breathlessly. 'Any hint it might be true – any sign at all?'

He shook his head. 'Nay, my friend. Though the old tales do tell that it is here, in the northern reaches, that the dragon lies, sleeping deep in the belly of the mountain. They say he has slumbered these five hundred spans and more, and will waken only when the True –' He stopped abruptly.

'When . . .' I prompted, without much hope that he'd continue. Truth was, I didn't need him to: I had a fair idea what he'd been going to say.

He shook his head, smiling grimly. 'I have said enough.'

'But do you think it's true – the legend of the dragon, I mean?'

'That I know not. But one thing I do know: there be no legend without the seed of truth at its beginning.'

'All the times you looked,' I said; 'the places you went . . . you must know these mountains better than almost anyone. Did you never find anywhere that looked even slightly promising?'

He thought for a moment, then smiled. 'There are nooks and crannies, gullies and ravines aplenty, both in this range and the main range to the west. But of all places, the one that gave me most hope lay to the far north – a place they call Brimstone Caverns. Skirt the mountains, then follow their foot westwards – you cannot mistake them. It is a long road, but the land is level and the route plain . . . and the mountains will shield you.'

'Shield us . . . from what?'

'From those who travel between Morningside and Dark Face.'

'Dark Face?'

'Aye.' His voice was grim. 'The far side of the mountains, where lies the new stronghold of King Karazeel – the Stronghold of Arraz. And now, I must bid you goodnight. May good fortune go with you, may the twin moons light your way . . .'

He clasped my wrist for a moment, then turned away. As he left, his stride quick and sure as he headed home, I heard – or thought I heard – *and may Zephyr guide your course.*

A BACKWARDS HORSERACE

'There you go – what did I tell you?' said Richard triumphantly. He was sprawled on his bed under the window of our attic room, chin in his hands. 'It *does* exist – and tomorrow we go dragon hunting!'

'It sounds like a long way, though,' said Gen. 'I have this feeling that time is creeping up behind us, closer and closer, without us knowing exactly when it's going to pounce – like a real-life game of K-I-N-G spells KING.'

Kenta made a face. 'I know just what you mean. But we can only do our best – and now, thanks to Adam, at least we have some idea where to start looking.'

Jamie was the only one already in bed, lying on his side with his blanket pulled up round his ears and his eyes screwed tight shut. 'Shush, you guys,' he said; 'I'm trying to sleep.'

'Well, I'm not,' said Gen, rolling over and staring up at the ceiling. 'Too much has happened today – my brain's buzzing.' She glanced over at Rich, his tousled blond hair a dusty gold in the moonlight that slanted through the window. 'Adam – give Richard the diary. We're getting so hung up on the dragon part of the poem that we're forgetting the rest – the *words of the past*. I want to know what happened about that horse race.'

Jamie's eyes popped open, and I saw he was as wide awake as any of us. There was a slightly queasy, preoccupied look on his face, as if he was scared he might be about to throw up and didn't want anyone to know. It was the thought of the morning, I realised suddenly – the dragon. He hadn't been trying to sleep; he'd been hiding behind his tightly closed eyelids. I had a niggling tug in the pit of my stomach too. It was all very well to hope that it wouldn't be a real dragon, but this was Karazan, where anything was possible.

Gen was right – it would be good to have a distraction from the thought of another long journey, and what might lie at the end of it. I passed the *Book of Days* across to Rich. He leafed through it, looking for the place Gen had left off the night before. Blue-bum sidled to the end of Kenta's bed and scrambled down, limped over to Richard's, and pulled himself up beside him. 'Look at little Blue-bum,' laughed Kenta. 'He wants to help, don't you? How I wish you could talk – you'd be full of good ideas.'

'Well, you can take your good ideas, along with your tail and blue bum, and shove off,' said Rich good-naturedly. 'It's my turn to read, and I don't need any help from anyone, thank you very much!'

There was a chorus of outrage from Jamie and the girls; Gen threw her pillow at Rich, and there was an energetic scuffle that stopped abruptly when Jamie pointed out the diary was in danger of getting crumpled.

At last everyone settled down again to listen. Propped on one elbow, waiting for Rich to find his place again and begin, I snuck a sidelong look at Blue-bum. He was huddled beside Kenta again, his back hunched, his beady eyes fixed intently on Rich. His gaze flicked over to me as if he could feel me watching him; he stretched his mouth into the familiar slit smile. I tried to smile back.

Had I imagined it? The look on Blue-bum's face when Rich made his ham-fisted but well-meaning retort: not the apologetic chittering grin I'd expected, but a red-eyed laser glare of rage.

The fourth day – the day of the Contest of Kings – was pronounced a holiday throughout Karazan. When the first grey light of dawn brushed the city walls to the south, they were already thronged with townsfolk well wrapped in their warmest cloaks, an excited babble of voices drowning out the chorus of the waking birds.

A silken tent had been set up on a low platform near the city gate for the royal party. Zaronel was carried to the pavilion in a litter, heavy velvet curtains concealing her from the people. The litter came to rest; the curtains were drawn back. Slowly, regally, Zaronel took up her place beside the mage, Zagros at her shoulder.

All was in readiness. Every eye was on the gate; every ear strained for the sound of hoof beats.

And here at last they came: the winged golden stallion of Prince Zane and the wild-eyed black mare of Prince Zeel, side by side. A roar went up from the people. The stallion threw up his head and leapt forward, snorting, foam flying from his bit. His rider jerked him back with hands of steel.

Zaronel's eyes widened.

The two horses paced nearer, approaching the platform from the east, silhouetted against the lightening sky.

The dawn gong boomed. The two horses sprang forward as one, their cloaked riders crouched low over their necks, driving them forward. The thunder of hooves dwindled into the distance as they rounded the edge of the forest and were gone.

Zaronel's heart beat at her breast like a trapped bird. She dared a glance at Meirion. He stood motionless, expressionless, his eyes closed.

Last will be first, first last . . .

Why then were the princes urging their horses on as if their very lives depended upon being first past the finish post?

A table had been set out on the grass before the platform. On its surface rested a single item: a golden bowl. The grassy swathe leading to it was lined with people, shouting and cheering, craning their necks for the first view of the returning horsemen.

Silence fell. In the silence, faint at first, came the rapid tattoo of hoof beats. Zaronel's own heart raced in time to their thunder as a great cry went up from the crowd and the first horse plunged into view, careering down the track towards the table at breakneck speed.

It was the black, hurtling down upon them like a thunderbolt.

And now in the distance the princess caught her first glimpse of the golden steed, far, so far behind . . .

The black was on them. It skidded into the turn, fighting for its head against the tight reins holding the reserves of strength and speed in check – for the race was only half run. The rider was half out of the saddle, tossing the golden leaf into the bowl . . . and they were away again on a hot gust of horse-sweat and leather, clods of earth kicking up onto the platform from the flying hooves.

But Zaronel had seen the rider's face . . . and at last she understood.

The prince whose horse is last across the finish line will win . . .

And now Prince Zane's winged stallion was upon them, eyes rolling white-rimmed, gouts of foam flying from his lips. The velvet corners of his mouth were jagged rips; bloody welts striped his flanks where the whip had split his satin hide. From a flat gallop the rider threw his full weight back on the reins, heaving at the horse's head with all his strength. The stallion slid sideways on his haunches and almost fell, throwing out his wings to save himself. Snarling, the horseman flung his crumpled golden leaf at the bowl, then jabbed his sharpened silver spurs into the horse's sides. The great beast lunged into a rearing run to escape the bite of the barbs – and they were gone.

The rider of the winged stallion was Zeel.

Princess Zaronel stared after them. Let it be the mare, *she prayed.* Let the black mare win.

The great crowd was silent. The minutes slipped by one by one, drops of water falling into a still pool. The future of Karazan, of Zaronel, of Antarion, hinged on which horse would come into view first.

The press of people hid the bend from sight. First came the hoof beats: then a long-drawn breath from the watchers, almost like a sigh.

As the horse came into sight, it seemed to Zaronel that it was moving in slow motion, its legs slicing through the air like swords, its head tossing and plunging like the crests of the white horses on the waves of the sea.

But this horse wasn't white. It was golden . . . it was winged . . . it was the stallion of Prince Zane, carrying his brother to victory.

Zaronel was seated upon a low stool in her chamber. She was awaiting Meirion, Prophet Mage of Karazan. As the sun set, he was to bring her the third gift: the gift of the new king. She waited, cold and still as marble, as the last rays of the sun faded and dusk crept into the chamber like a thief.

The knock came; the door opened. Meirion was there, hands outstretched. His eyes smiled down at her. On his palms rested a single scarlet rose.

The room swam; warm blood rushed to her face. 'I – I do not understand,' *she faltered.* 'Prince Zeel . . . the race . . .'

'My dear princess,' Meirion's voice was very gentle, 'the

ways of Karazan are seldom simple; as queen, you will
come to understand them better with time. There was
not one test, but three. The first: to win your heart. The
second: to unravel the riddle of the race. The third: the
race itself.' He paused, and a shadow fell over his face.
'On the second lap, hidden from view of the watchers,
Prince Zeel flew the golden stallion, keeping low, under
cover of the trees. He overtook the black and won the race,
but he did so by deceit and trickery. Of this, Prince Zane
told me nothing. But the Oracle . . . the Oracle sees
with the inner eye, though sometimes through a veil of
darkness.

'Some things can be seen and yet not changed, Princess
Zaronel of Karazan; and some things, alas, cannot be
seen.'

He left, closing the door softly behind him.

When the second knock came, Zaronel was sitting at the
window, gazing at the rose. With the falling darkness its
colour had bled away; it was a grey flower in a grey hand.

'Enter,' she called softly.

The dark shape of Zeel blocked the doorway.

'One day,' he hissed, 'one day, Zaronel of Antarion,
you will be mine – you, and the crown you bring with you.
On that day every horse in Karazan will be butchered and
the carcasses burned; the smoke will cover the sky and blot
out the stars.

'Wait . . . and watch.'

THE BRIMSTONE CAVERNS

We left Drakendale before sunrise, breakfasting on stale leftover bread in the foothills overlooking Marshall. The last time we'd looked down from here a wall of shroud had loomed up to touch the sky, blocking any view of what lay beyond. Now that was gone. Beyond the deserted town the endless swamp stretched like shattered shards of glass, and it was the white glare of the horizon that hid the fortress of Shakesh from view.

We saw no sign of life, either in Marshall or on the rough, marshy grassland that skirted the foothills. When Danon had talked of roads and routes I'd had a mental image of a track, or at least a path. But there was nothing. Taking turns with Rich to lead the way, I thought how strange it was to be so completely alone, our only guide the string of mountains we were following, and the slow journey of the sun as we followed it into the west.

At nightfall of the first day we camped in the shadow of a vast mountain that reared up to dwarf the rest, its peak lost in cloud. We could make out another, almost as tall, half-hidden behind it. Gazing up at them, I felt a sinking sense of despair: even with Danon's help, how would we ever find a dragon in such vastness, if one existed – let alone a prince? And if we did – what then? Would Zephyr know what to do? Would he have an army in hiding, ready to come at his call? Most of all, would he be in time . . . would we?

That night there was no moon. A corrugated blanket of black cloud stretched across the sky; thunder rolled and rumbled round the mountaintops, sheets of lightning washing the plain with pale, bluish light. We huddled round the campfire, silent and exhausted, waiting for rain that never came. There was no mention of the diary or our quest; of dragons or princes, real or legendary. But I noticed that I wasn't the only one who kept glancing up, wondering what might be wheeling, unseen, above the clouds.

Towards evening of the second day Rich gave a hoarse shout and broke into a stumbling run. Jolted out of the daze I'd been walking in I stared round me, wondering what he'd seen; then jogged reluctantly after him, tuning out Jamie's familiar wail of 'Wait up, guys – not so fast!'

The gentle foothills we'd been following had given way to steep cliffs – not the sheer, granite-like rock of the Cliffs of Stone, but rough pumice that spilled onto the ground under our feet like a rumpled sheet of sandpaper. Stubborn tufts of pale grass grew here and there, clinging grimly to invisible pockets of earth blown by the wind from whatever lay to the north. Ahead of me, Rich had disappeared round a rocky outcrop. I followed, panting, the lead weight of Blue-bum jouncing on my back; rounded the corner – and stopped dead in my tracks.

Danon had been right: there was no mistaking them.

The misty evening sunlight fell full on a massive steeply sloping cliff face, wrinkled and pleated as if long ago the rock had been liquid mud. Where the cliff met the ground it cut sharply backwards into the rock in a deep, shallow gash almost like a low room, its roof as high as my head. A jagged barrier of strange, pointed rock formations straggled up from the floor of the overhang and down from the edge of the roof like snaggled teeth guarding a shark's open mouth.

Above the shallow cave the cliff face reared up to meet the sky – and there, close to the top and side by side in the rock, gaped two huge caves. They stared out over the plain like great eyes looking endlessly into the distance, seeing everything – or nothing. Above the edge of the cliff I could just make out the distant tips of the two mountains we'd passed the day before, side by side, covered in snow.

Behind me, I heard Jamie groan.

I slipped Kenta's pack off my aching shoulders and lowered it gently to the ground, loosening the top so Blue-bum could scramble out; found my water bottle and took a long swallow. Rich had been clambering about on the flange of rock above the low cave; now he jumped down and came over to us, dusting off his hands and holding them up for us to see. They were covered in tiny pockmarks like measles.

He was grinning. 'The rock's hard on your hands, but dead easy to climb – there are heaps of hand- and footholds. How about that? We've found them – the Brimstone Caverns! That bottom one's a dud – it just slopes lower and lower till it meets the ground right at the back – but the top two are made to measure. What was it again? *In empty sockets seek the prize . . .*'

'*That's hidden in the dragon's eyes*,' quavered Jamie.

'If those aren't empty sockets,' said Gen, 'I don't know what are.'

'Which means . . .' said Kenta.

'Which means . . . ' gulped Jamie.

'Which means the dragon's in there! Way to go, Danon!' whooped Rich. 'So up we go – sooner the better, while it's still light. What d'you say, guys? Coming?'

I glanced at the sun, hesitating. It was very low now, almost on the horizon. In an hour at the most, it would be dark. But on the other hand, in a few minutes the sun would be shining almost directly into the caves. If we went quickly and made use of the natural light, it would be easier than trying to make do with torches.

'I guess so,' I said, but there was a hollow, slightly sick feeling in the pit of my stomach. 'Jamie? Girls? How about it?'

Jamie stared up at the cliff. So did I. I thought of him way high, flattened against the rock, his chubby fingers clinging to the holds. Thought of his voice drifting through the stillness into the listening depths of the caves: *Wait up, guys! Wait up!*

The silence stretched thinner and thinner, like a piece of chewing gum.

'Though we need to find some wood for a fire,' I said slowly, as if I was thinking aloud. 'I don't know about the rest of you, but Barbecue Beef with Beans sounds good to me. So if you'd like to stay and help the girls with dinner, Jamie . . .'

Two minutes later we'd thrown the few remaining bits and pieces out of Kenta's pack and loaded it with climbing essentials: water, torches, rope.

While the girls weren't watching, Rich slipped in his pocket knife, 'just in case'.

If he meant 'just in case we meet the dragon', I sure hoped it turned out to be a small one.

Standing in the soft warmth of the evening sun, it seemed impossible. But boosting myself up onto the floor of the cavern, it felt very different.

From the ground I'd imagined the cave like an enormous hall, bright and open, the sun beaming in right to the very back. But the climb took longer than we'd expected, and by the time we finally reached the cave the sun had almost disappeared. It was still light enough to see our way, but it was a dusty, diffused kind of light, as if the ordinary sunlight had been crumbled into dust and mixed with darkness.

Slowly, cautiously, Rich and I picked our way across the lumpy, uneven floor. Stubby stalagmites poked up here and there, casting crooked shadows like bony fingers pointing the way. It wasn't long before the cave began to narrow and darken, buttresses and bends blocking out the remaining light. 'Look,' whispered Rich. Echoes of his voice came back at us from every side, as if there were mocking watchers in the shadows. He pointed. A tunnel led off to the right, leading back the way we'd come. 'I bet that leads to the other cave. They join up, then go deeper into the mountainside. Awesome, huh?' His eyes gleamed in the gloom.

Huh – huh – huh – huh – huh. The echoes eddied round us like hollow laughter.

Ahead the tunnel narrowed, stretching on and downwards into the darkness.

I wanted to go back. 'Rich,' I began; 'd'you think –'

'Shhhh. We don't want him to hear us. No more talking. We use hand signals from now on, OK? And when we find him, we'll creep as close as we can . . .'

I felt as if my guts were melting. As we groped in the bag for our torches, I wondered if Rich was completely crazy. Or maybe to him, it was just a wonderful game. I trailed miserably after him, my hands slick with sweat, my heart thudding in a slow, painful rhythm, wishing I was half as brave.

INTO THE DARKNESS

Soon it was pitch dark. I shone the dim beam of my torch on Rich's feet and followed, treading as softly as I could. The heels of his boots were worn right down, and the stitching in the leather was starting to come away. I found the sight of the worn rubber and frayed thread oddly comforting.

I could hear the soft huff of Richard's breathing and smell him ahead of me in the darkness: a familiar, comforting mixture of sweaty feet and unwashed skin. I was sweating too. It was getting hotter. Down and down we went, deeper and deeper into the heart of the mountain. I wondered how far Danon had come, all those years ago when he was a boy . . .

Something brushed against my hair. I flinched, biting back a yell, and shone my torch upwards. It was the tunnel roof; I could feel its enormous weight pressing down on me. The beam flashed into a deep fissure just ahead and I glimpsed a clump of bony, hunched shapes clinging like dried carcasses to the rock, shuffling and twitching in the light. I jerked the torch away, ducked low and hurried on.

Soon we were stooped almost double. My back was on fire; I would have given anything just to stand straight and stretch and feel the sun on my skin. Up ahead, Rich had dropped to his hands and knees; I caught a momentary flash of white as his grin lit the darkness. *Yeah, Rich: fun and games*, I thought grimly as I crawled after him. *One good thing: if there is a dragon down here, it can't be much bigger than a parrot.*

We must have been nearly back at ground level when Rich stopped, so suddenly I knocked into him. It was boiling hot and so stuffy I could hardly breathe. The trapped, claustrophobic feeling was worse. All I wanted was out of there. I waited, panting, shining my torch on his broad backside, praying he'd give whatever hand signal meant *dead end – head back*.

Instead, I heard a sound: a peculiar liquid lapping. My heart roller-coastered, skidding on adrenaline. What was down here, licking at Rich in the dark? The dragon?

Then Rich spoke: a whisper of sound harsh as a shout in the closeness of the tunnel. 'It's water. Hot.'

Relief coursed through me. *We've reached the end. We can go back.* But then there was a sloshing sound. Rich, crawling forward into the water.

I followed him. There was nothing else I could do.

He was right, the water was hot. Like bath water, but with a tinny, rotten-egg smell that made me think Rich had done a fart. It got steadily deeper, the tunnel roof lowering to meet it. And still Rich crawled on.

At last, when the water was up to my chest, he

stopped again. I'd been holding my torch in my mouth like a dog with a bone; it was covered in spit. I shone it forwards. That was it. Dead end. A stubby wall of black rock dipped down to meet black water. Goodbye, Brimstone Caverns.

Rich was patting away at the rock face, like he was hoping to find a hidden switch that would open a secret door. I shook my head, not knowing whether to feel angry or frustrated or admiring, or all three. The guy was nuts.

He handed me the pack. 'Wait for me here, Adam. I'm going in.' *What? In where?* Before I understood what he was on about – way before I could even begin to stop him – there was a splash and a gurgle, a stream of rotten-egg bubbles, and Rich was gone. I was staring at the fuzzy splodge of torchlight on rock, completely alone. I said the worst word I knew three times, loudly. I didn't give a toss if the dragon heard.

I turned off my torch and shoved it into my pocket, and put the pack on a rocky ledge safely above the water. Felt my way to the wall, down into the water. The floor dropped into nothingness; I could feel a sharp angle where the roof began again a ruler-length down. Like a gigantic step . . . a vertical kink in the tunnel, taking it underwater – and then where? A step up again into the dragon's lair? Another step down, and down, and down, into drowning blackness? Or just on and on, under the water, breath burning and lungs bursting, till you couldn't hold your breath any more . . .

What if Rich gave up and turned back, and met me head-on in the tunnel?

What if there was something down there in the black water?

What if Rich needed help?

I took a deep, deep breath, closed my eyes on the blackness, and squiggled forward and under the rim of rock, down under the water, and into the tunnel.

I swam with both hands at full stretch, feet kicking along behind. The water was hot – so hot I could feel my eyeballs swelling and my eardrums bulging. My head was bumping against the roof; the toes of my boots scuffed the bottom with every kick. My heart pumped huger than the tunnel, squeezing me along like toothpaste in a tube. I felt my lungs starting to burn, a steel fist gripping them tighter, tighter . . . Where was Rich? Should I turn back? Could I – was there room? If I did, would I have enough breath to get back? Now panic was fluttering at the base of my brain – beating its wings harder, faster – a frantic drumming in time with my heart . . .

Then the roof was gone; my head burst up through the water, and red light blinded me. I squatted knee-deep, my arm shielding my face, sucking in air.

Slowly I lowered my arm and looked.

Richard was crouched at the edge of the water. He put the finger and thumb of one hand in a circle. What did that mean? Put the other index finger to his lips. I knew that one, but I didn't need telling. Then linked his thumbs and flapped his hands. *Dragon*. Gave a wobbly grin.

The tunnel was wide, washed with the faint, reddish glow that had blinded me when I'd first emerged from the blackness of the water. It angled away from us, up and right, round a sharp bend and out of sight.

The dragon was all round us. Its breath fanned my face with a fiery flush I could see mirrored on Richard's, dripping and steaming. Its stench caught in my throat like smoke: the same sulphur, rotten-egg reek of the water. Its breathing echoed everywhere – hoarse, snoring breaths interspersed with deep belches and hiccuping, bubbling gulps. Jamie had been wrong. The dragon was real. I'd been wrong too. It wasn't as big as a parrot. It was as big as a mountain.

Richard and I looked at each other. I didn't need hand signals to know what he was thinking. I was thinking it too. *We can go back right now, and no one will ever know.*

Round the corner, the dragon gurgled and slurped.

As softly as I could, I straightened and stepped out of the water, leaving wet footprints on the rock behind me. Moved up beside Rich, in utter silence. Pointed at my chest; then at the bend in the tunnel. Thumbs-up. Tried to smile. *I'll go – I'll be fine. Can't wait.* But my face had turned to cardboard, so maybe the last part of the message didn't get through. A hot, wet hand gripped mine like a vice. Rich grinned back – more of a snarl than a grin. The ultimate hand signal.

We're in this together.

Hand in hand like kindergarten kids, hearts thumping like drums, we crept to the corner and peered round.

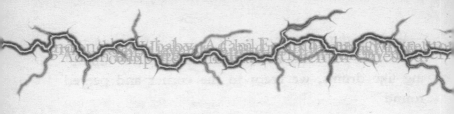

THE BELLY OF THE BEAST

Heat hit me in the face like a fist. I reeled, groping for my cloak with my free hand and clamping it over my nose and mouth. It was sodden and dripping, cool as a forest stream compared to the burning air searing my lungs.

The dragon – where was the dragon?

I stared wildly round the cavern that had opened out before us. It was vast as a cathedral, every corner lit by a pulsating red glow that ebbed and flowed like the beat of a massive heart. There were no shadows; nowhere for even the smallest creature to creep away and hide.

Where was it?

It was everywhere – yet it was nowhere. Reflections of its fiery breath flickered on the walls and licked the roof with crimson. Its choking stink scorched my throat. Its breathing echoed from every corner, rolling round the colossal hall like thunder. But it wasn't the snoring of a creature asleep: it was the gulping slaver of a monster devouring its prey.

The heat was searing my brain; I couldn't think.

I squinted down the length of the cave. It extended away from us into the distance, at least four times as long as it was wide. Down its centre, in the rock floor, gaped a gigantic fissure. It was as if a pair of giant hands had gripped the floor and ripped it open: an irregular rent stretching from one end of the cave to the other.

The bubbling sound and the red glow – hot and bright as a hundred suns – was coming from the crack. As I stared at it, eyeballs frazzling, a spray of brilliant sparks, white-hot, burning-blue and gold, shot up like a fountain and fell back again, a few droplets splashing to land like liquid rubies on the jagged rim of rock.

And then I knew.

I tightened my grip on Richard's hand and drew him back into the tunnel; back to where the water waited for us, spilled ink on the dark rock. He stared at me, eyes puffy and bloodshot, hair sticking up in crazy tufts. 'Where is it?' he croaked. 'The dragon?'

'There isn't one. What we found . . . it's the heart of the mountain. Its molten core.' My throat felt raw; tasted tinny, like blood. 'I guess people would have thought – long ago – a dragon lived in the mountains. Because of the fire and stuff. *There be no legend without the seed of truth at its beginning*. But that's all it is: a legend.'

'It can't be just a legend!' objected Jamie in a furious squeak. 'There must be *some* kind of dragon, *somewhere*. The poem – the prophecy poem – it *can't* be wrong: it's *magic*!'

I couldn't help smiling to myself as I scraped the last smears of gravy from my plate with my finger and sucked it clean. For someone who hadn't believed in magic a short while ago, Jamie had developed touching faith in it.

'Are you absolutely certain there wasn't a dragon anywhere in that cave?' asked Gen for what seemed the millionth time. 'A tiny one, maybe – hiding away in a corner?'

'Yes, Gen,' I said patiently; 'I'm absolutely sure.'

'And he'd put it on tape for you if we had one – save him telling you over and over again,' growled Rich.

'*In empty sockets seek the prize that's hidden in the dragon's eyes*,' said Jamie sadly. 'And we're really saying – for definite – that it's a dud?'

I stared into the fire. The flames seemed dim beside my memory of the hidden inferno deep in the belly of the mountain. Could it really mean nothing? 'I'm afraid so.'

'Then what are we left with?' asked Gen. 'We're back to *pools of darkness* again – and we still haven't the least idea where they might be.'

'Yeah – pity you didn't think to ask Danon about them while you were about it,' grumbled Rich.

'And *words of the past*. We haven't learned much from the diary so far, though,' said Kenta, gathering up the dishes. 'I know it's your turn to clear, Adam, but you've done enough today. You two look terrible.'

But I was on my feet in a second, jelly legs and all. 'Hey, Weevil – Blue-bum, I mean – where d'you think you're going?' He was sidling over to my pack, keeping to the shadows at the edge of the firelight. He looked across at Kenta, cringing and chittering.

'Don't yell at him, Adam! He's trying to help by fetching the diary for us – aren't you, Blue-bum?' said Kenta. 'Give it to him, Adam – let him bring it across to me. He just wants to do his share.'

'Hardly a share,' muttered Rich. 'How about letting *him* clear away, if he's so keen to be helpful?'

'It's OK – I've got it. Here you go, Kenta.' For some reason I didn't like the thought of Weevil touching the diary. I forced the feeling down, pasting a stiff smile on my face. 'Thanks, Blue-bum. Sorry to growl. I'm just tired, I guess.'

'Now, where were we up to?' Kenta opened the little book, tilting it so the moonlight fell on the pages. 'The coronation . . .'

Blue-bum scrambled onto her lap and peered down at the page, then up at her face. Chattered softly; then reached out a tiny, crooked paw and scrabbled at the paper.

I said nothing.

'What is it, Blue-bum? What are you trying to tell me? You want to turn over? You think we should read further on?' There was a volley of staccato clicks from Blue-bum. Kenta looked up at us. 'Blue-bum thinks we should read further on,' she announced. 'And you know: he's right. It's a really good idea.'

247

'Yes,' said Gen slowly. 'I guess it is. I don't know why we didn't think of it before.'

'We need to know what happened to Zane . . .' said Jamie.

'And what happened to Zephyr after that. Let me see if I can find anything . . .' Kenta flipped through the pages, frowning.

Blue-bum looked across at me and stretched his mouth into a smug monkey-smile. I pretended not to notice. He was right. We needed to get to the guts of what had happened fifty years ago – and we had no time to lose. There was a funny, hollow feeling inside me that I thought must be relief. Of course Blue-bum was still on our side. He wanted Zephyr found as much as anyone – and this proved it.

'Wait a second,' said Kenta suddenly. 'This part here – the writing changes. It's not Zaronel any more. It's Zagros. Listen to this:

'*I am Zagros, warrior lord, Guardian of the Jewel of Antarion. I write in moonlight, for my lady cannot . . .*'

FLOWERS OF SCARLET

*F*ive long years had passed since the twisted crowns
had been placed on the heads of King Zane
and Queen Zaronel, and the Sign of Sovereignty
set upon the new king's hand. It was a golden era for
Karazan and her sister state Antarion; a time of peace and
prosperity.

Now at last, after years of waiting, had come the most
joyous tidings of all. The belly of Queen Zaronel was ripe
with child. The prince – for none were in any doubt that
the baby would be a boy – was to be borne on the wings of
the Zephyr, the southerly wind that tipped the balance
of the seasons from the warm days of summer to the long
dark nights of winter.

It should have been a time of perfect happiness. Yet a
shadow lay over Arakesh; a feeling of foreboding, as if a
nameless evil lurked in some hidden place. Zagros felt it,
and he knew his lady felt it also, though she did not speak
of it.

But King Zane did not. His footfalls rang on the
flagstones as he ran up the winding stairway to his wife;
his laughter rang out like a bell as he knelt before her, his

palms spread on her stomach, feeling the strong legs of his son kick against his hands; the soft lullaby of his larigot drifted from the window of the royal bedchamber each night as he played queen and unborn prince to sleep.

Zagros kept as closely as he could to Zaronel's side. Only when King Zane was beside her in the Summer Palace did he relax his vigilance. Even at night, he kept his place outside their door. And his keen eyes watched.

Especially they watched Prince Zeel, who it seemed had a new stillness since the news of the baby prince. He smiled more, but something about the smile put Zagros in mind of the serpents in the sacred temple, with their flat, watchful eyes.

It was the custom of King Zane and Queen Zaronel to hold court on the golden afternoons in the great hall. There, on matching thrones, they would listen to the petitions of their people; or rather King Zane would listen, nodding, smiling, sometimes frowning, always just and fair in his pronouncements. Queen Zaronel would sit quietly by, head bent over whatever sewing, crochet or tapestry her hands were busy with, directing the occasional smiling glance or soft word of counsel to her king.

Of late her nimble fingers had been busy with the preparation of a layette for the baby prince: garment after garment of softest cotton and delicate lambswool, all in purest white or cream: nightgowns; tiny leggings and bonnets; little jackets with buttons of pearl; fluffy blankets and lacy shawls to swaddle the newborn.

And always, Zagros stood a pace behind the queen's throne, and watched.

Now, two neighbours who had been locked in a bitter dispute over a boundary fence were leaving the hall. Ten minutes before, guards had restrained them from settling the matter with fists and daggers; now, following the counsel of the king, they were leaving, arm in arm and laughing, to celebrate the renewal of their friendship at the tavern.

King Zane lifted a pewter tankard of water to his lips and took a long draught, then stretched, yawning. 'It has been a long afternoon, Meirion. How many more?'

The mage consulted the scroll that lay on the oak pedestal before him, concealing a smile in his beard. He knew that the hours spent at Citizen's Council did not sit comfortably on the shoulders of the young king, who regarded them in the same light as he did parchment and quill: a necessary hardship. 'Only one, my lord.'

Zane met his wife's eyes in a shared glance of rueful resignation. Smiling, Zaronel snipped a loose end of snow-white wool with a pair of tiny golden scissors and held up the finished garment for him to see. It was a tiny sock, edged with frothy lace and threaded at the ankle with a satin ribbon. Taking it from her, the king slipped the sock carefully over the top of one large brown thumb. It barely fitted. King Zane examined it solemnly. 'This is an exquisite piece of craftsmanship, my beloved Zara,' he pronounced at last with great solemnity. 'But dare I ask the question: is it a fitting boot for the mighty foot of the future King of the United Empires?' He passed it back with a laugh, and she placed it with the other finished articles in the sandalwood box beside her throne.

The king sighed. 'Very well, Meirion: send him in.'

At a signal from the mage a figure appeared at the far end of the long carpet, and made its way slowly towards the thrones.

He was a man of middle years, clad in a ragged leather jerkin and blood-stained breeches. As he drew nearer, Zagros heard Zaronel draw in her breath; saw her put her hand up to her throat. The man's face was disfigured by a raw, weeping wound: a gash that ran from eye to chin, crusted with blood and yellow pus and blue with bruising at its edges.

'My lord king,' said Zaronel softly, 'this man should have been sent to the Temple for healing before seeking audience here.'

Before the king could reply the man himself spoke, falling to his knees on the low step in front of the thrones.

'Good King Zane,' he said, his voice hollow with exhaustion and pain, 'I beg you for help. I am a wood-cutter in the Forests of Nightshade: I dwell with wife and children in a village that numbers no more than two dozen souls. Our lives are humble; we wish for nothing but to live in peace and safety. But now . . .'

'Now?'

'Now a creature is come more fearsome than any from myth or legend. A giant boar, taller than a horse and more massive than a bull. Its tusks are as long as my forearm and sharper than swords; its appetite is for human flesh, and cannot be sated. Two days past the men of our

village – six in number – tried to hunt it down. Two are dead; one will not live to see the dawn. Our women and children cower behind barred doors by day, and cannot sleep at night for the terrors that come to them in their dreams. I beseech you for aid, my lord king, before all is lost.'

In one swift stride King Zane was beside him, raising him gently to his feet. 'Beg no more. Come, stand tall and be of good cheer. Mage Meirion will take you and minister to your wounds; he will give you a phial of healing potion for your friend, and food and wine. Before nightfall a party of hunters will set forth to track this monster and destroy it. Have no fear: they will not rest until the task is done. As your king I am pledged to do all in my power to rid Karazan of its ancient legacy of evil, whatever form it may take. Remember that in the kingdom of Karazan you are never alone: the might of the crown and the power of good stand always at your shoulder.'

'And why do we not join the chase, brother?' Zagros' eyes flicked to the doorway. Zeel stood there, his customary black garb almost concealing him in the shadows, his dark-cloaked steward as always by his side. Zeel stepped forward, smiling. 'It is long since we hunted together, Zane. This beast sounds a worthy quarry. Or are you now too much the king to bloody your hands at the kill?'

Zane turned to Zaronel, and Zagros saw the wild light of the hunter burning in his eyes like a bright flame. She said nothing. She looked steadily into the eyes of her lord: a long, level look that had no need of words.

King Zane shuffled his feet and flushed; looked down,

then darted a cautious, hopeful glance at her face. 'Come, Zara,' he coaxed; 'it would not be long. It is a fortnight yet till we expect the arrival of our small stranger.' Then he smiled, a boyish grin that lit his face like sunlight, and Zagros knew that his lady was lost. 'Let me go – this last time. Then I will be glad to put the thrill of the hunt aside for a while. You have my word.'

Zaronel smiled back at him. It was only Zagros who saw the shadow of fear suddenly deepen in her eyes . . . and noted the soft departure of the servant Evor as he hobbled swiftly away in the direction of his turret room.

The party of hunters left as the sun was setting, the woodcutter riding a pace or two behind King Zane on a borrowed horse. The deep voices of the men and the jingle of harness carried clearly through the still air to Queen Zaronel, standing with one hand on the cold stone of the battlements, the other pressed to the swell beneath her bosom. 'Well, Zagros?' she asked, knowing he would be there without needing to turn. 'Will he be long?'

Zagros did not reply. Like Zaronel, he was watching for the king to turn as he always did, brush a kiss to his fingertips, and blow it up to where his lady waited. But the king's horse was fresh and itching to run; laughing, he held the prancing stallion back, calling over his shoulder to his companions, and did not turn.

It was Zeel who turned back, his pale, empty eyes seeking out the silent figure of Zaronel, grey as a ghost on the high tower as evening fell about her.

★

254

A week passed, and the hunting party did not return. Eight days; nine, and still no word. Each sunrise, Zagros followed Zaronel to the high tower that faced to the west, and gazed with her over the empty darkness of the forest. Zaronel asked that a chair be placed in the shelter of the battlements in the sunshine, and there she sat by day, her hands idle in her lap, staring into the trees.

They came on the evening of the thirteenth day. Zaronel sat alone in the vast dining hall, at the foot of the long table. As always, a rich feast was spread before her, but she had eaten nothing.

The great studded door burst open. Zeel stood framed in the doorway, his pale eyes fixed on her face like leeches. 'It is done.'

Zaronel half-rose, then sank back in her chair as if she no longer had the strength to stand. She was pale as death. 'Where is he?'

There was a silence. Then Zeel smiled. 'My brother is here. But alas, he is . . . indisposed. Something he has eaten, perhaps.' He raised one hand and clicked his fingers. Still, his eyes did not leave Zaronel's face.

Two of Zeel's servants appeared in the doorway. Between them hung the tall figure of King Zane, an arm round each of their necks. Instantly, Zagros sprang forward, taking the weight of the king, pushing the sly-eyed footmen aside. His gaze was fixed on the face of his king; had Evor been hovering in the shadows, he would not have seen him.

The king was utterly changed. His skin had a greenish pallor and gleamed with a sheen of greasy sweat. His hair hung in oily ropes. He had about him an odd, fungal smell, like rotten mushrooms. His eyes were rolled up in their sockets, and a thin string of saliva hung from his slack mouth.

'Call Meirion.' Zagros growled the words as he lowered his lord as gently as a baby into the great throne at the head of the table. A tremor ran through the body of the king; his eyes jerked open and fastened on Zaronel's ashen face.

'My love . . .'

Zaronel's face was frozen; it did not change. But Zagros' heart gave a great leap in his chest, as if it were about to burst apart. 'FETCH MEIRION!' he bellowed.

King Zane's eyes were pools of blood.

If Evor melted silently from the room, no one saw him go.

Slowly, slowly, as if it was weighted down with a steel gauntlet almost too heavy to lift, King Zane reached out his hand towards Zaronel. He gave a single, soft cough.

A fountain of drops as bright as rubies sprayed over the polished wood of the table, over the platters of fruit and sweetmeats and plaited bread and pastries, over the silver and crystal and the spotless brocade of the napkins.

It splashed the breast and swollen belly of the queen with flowers of scarlet, as if her own heart had been pierced with a mortal wound.

TAPESTRIES OF DESTINY

I woke while it was still dark and lay watching the stars fade in the lightening sky. The words of the past had woven their way through my dreams; now their invisible threads drifted in the soft light of dawn like a cobweb spun across time, fragile strands connecting the past to the present with a symmetry I didn't begin to understand.

Soon, Karazeel had said. How soon was soon? We'd been in Karazan for days, and we were no nearer finding Zephyr than when we'd first arrived. It seemed to me that we were blundering round blindly, occasionally stumbling into things that should have helped us – would have helped us, if we knew what they meant.

'It's like doing a jigsaw puzzle: all the pieces are on the table, staring us in the face, and we just can't fit them together,' Gen agreed over breakfast.

'Let's go over what we've got, and what we know,' Jamie suggested. 'Bags I go first. We've got Queen Zaronel's magic diary.'

'And we know that King Zane was taken ill on a

hunting trip just before Zephyr was born –' said Kenta.

'Poisoned, I reckon,' interrupted Rich. 'By Zeel, and that sidekick of his, Evor. Slimy toad.'

'We've got that cylinder thing,' continued Jamie doubtfully, 'from the secret passage in the Summer Palace – remember?'

'But we don't know what it is.'

'And we've got a bottle of totally useless furniture oil,' said Rich.

'And a gold coin . . .'

'And a handful of loose change . . .'

'And a magic map,' I said.

'And a poem that's supposedly the key to it all – if only we could understand it,' finished Gen.

'A poem that's a load of twaddle, you mean,' grumbled Rich. 'The dragon part at least.'

'And time is running out,' I said reluctantly. 'It has to be.'

There was a gloomy silence.

'Let's have a look at where we're at – literally,' said Jamie at last. 'Haul out the map, Kenta.'

'I haven't got it. I took everything out, remember – to make room for Blue-bum.'

'So who has?'

'Me.' My pack was a dumping-ground for every-thing no one else wanted to carry; most of the things Kenta had offloaded had found their way into it, map and parchment included. But I didn't mind a bit of extra weight, and years of Matron and Highgate had trained me to keep everything tidily stowed away in its proper place. Ask me where anything in that pack was, and I'd be able to tell you exactly.

But now, my bag was a mess. Someone had been through it while I was asleep, or off looking for wood. Had it been Kenta, hunting for matches to start the fire? Or . . .

Suddenly I froze. My shawl was damp.

Our bags were completely waterproof. So how . . . Frowning, I pulled the shawl out and sniffed it. It smelled the way pine trees do after rain. I groped for the bottle of revealing oil Danon had given me; pulled it out, upside-down. Minus the cork. Empty.

Luckily the diary had been right at the top – though that wasn't where I'd left it last night. Kenta had given it back to me once the moon had disappeared and she'd had to stop reading; I'd tucked it down the side, into its special place next to my penny whistle.

But just about everything else in the bag was soaked and stank of resin. I could feel a sick, familiar anger bubbling up inside me like bile. It was a feeling I hadn't had since those long-ago days at Highgate, with Weevil.

But this wasn't Highgate, and it wasn't Weevil sitting on his haunches watching me with bright, beady eyes. This was Karazan, and that was Blue-bum, and everything was different . . . wasn't it?

Even without unrolling it, I could tell the map was wrecked. It had soaked the oil up like a sponge. Before, the parchment had been thick and creamy;

now it was translucent and shiny like greaseproof paper. The ink would be totally smudged.

I unrolled it gently and smoothed it flat. I'd been wrong: it wasn't smudged. But it looked different – way different. It took me a moment to figure out why. 'The splodge,' I said slowly. 'The splodge has completely disappeared. Danon's revealing oil – it's revealed the whole map!'

We must have wasted at least half an hour huddled over the map, exclaiming over the mountains and forests and rivers and towns that had been hidden before. Everything was marked: everywhere we'd been, and everywhere – like the Stronghold of Arraz – we knew that thankfully we'd never have to go.

But something was nibbling at the edges of my mind. I let the others' excited chatter flow over me, and tried to pin it down. What was it Kai was always saying? *There be patterns in the tapestries of destiny, yet those caught in the weave find those patterns hard to see.* That meant things happened for a purpose. There'd been a piece missing in the jigsaw – or a piece we hadn't seen. Now, suddenly, an accident had revealed the whole map of Karazan. An accident – or destiny?

I stared down at the map. It was like a tapestry, intricate and detailed. Could there be something on the map we were missing – that we were too close to the weave to see? Like that long-ago clue in the dark chamber of the Temple of Arakesh: the clue that had revealed the Serpent of Power. The black serpent

whose coils had padded the entire circumference of the room, *too vast to notice* . . . Were we so focused on detail that we were missing something that was quite literally staring us in the face?

And then I saw it. The dragon *was* real.

It wasn't as big as a parrot, and it wasn't as big as a mountain.

The dragon was the entire Draken Mountain range: the whole vast chain, stretching like a sleeping giant from its snaggle-toothed head in the north to where the curve of its spined tail dwindled away to low hills in the far south.

THE EYES OF THE DRAGON

The climb up to the plateau was easier than any of us expected, but it took forever. The girls insisted on roping us all together for safety, though Rich said that just meant that if one of us fell, we all would. But it was just as well – without the security of the nylon rope knotted tightly round him, I doubt Jamie would have managed to get even halfway up the cliff.

By the time we finally hoisted him over the top the sun was overhead and we were drenched in sweat. If we'd been expecting a view, we were disappointed. We were on a broad, high saddle, a dipped hummock of flat ground slung between the two low ridges. They rose up on either side in a jagged rim, hiding the plains to the north and the valley we now knew lay to the south. That valley was the Cauldron of Zeel, guarded by the snarling face and razor teeth of the dragon on one side, its flexed foreleg and curved claws on the other . . . and in its centre lay the new fortress of King Karazeel, the Stronghold of Arraz.

But all we could see was the long plain stretching

away from us, ripples of scaly grey bedrock stippled with patches of blue-green tussock and shallow drifts of fine, dry sand. Far ahead the two snow-topped mountains towered above the plateau, floating weightlessly on a shimmering haze of heat; to their right the peaks of the dragon's back curved away into the mists of the far distance.

The ground was firm and dry underfoot; birds twittered and spun in the still air. Best of all, we knew that finally we were on the right track, and must be nearing the end of our quest.

Rich wiped his forehead on his sleeve and took a noisy swig from his canteen. 'I vote we head straight for the base of the two mountains,' he said, pointing. 'See how they stick up from the dragon's head like ears? You don't need to be a genius to work out that somewhere between us and them will be the dragon's eyes. We don't even need to bother about the pools of darkness and the empty sockets. We've cut straight to the chase: I'm betting the dragon's eyes will be caves, and that's where Zephyr and his army will be holed up – in the perfect position to crash down on old Karazeel like a ton of bricks!'

We tramped on through the long afternoon and into the evening. The mountains were further away than they looked, and at times it felt as if we were marking time, walking on the spot without making any progress. I found my mind drifting, lulled by the swinging rhythm of my stride. And always, my gaze and my thoughts returned to the bulge of Blue-bum, snoozing away at the bottom of the pack on Rich's back.

I wished my feelings about him were simple and straightforward, like the others' seemed to be. But I couldn't help wondering if it had been him who'd rifled through my bag . . . and whether it had been an accident that the revealing oil had spilled over the map. Was Blue-bum trying to help us? Had he somehow guessed – or known – what the lotion would reveal? He was more capable than any of us of figuring it out – as Weevil, he'd been super-smart. But why not find a more direct way of telling us?

There was still so much I didn't understand. But as the afternoon wore on and the mountains grew from misty silhouettes to rearing walls of rock and scree, I realised it wasn't important. By tonight – tomorrow at the latest – we'd be home, and none of it would matter.

The terrain sloped gradually upwards, growing rougher and more rugged as we neared the mountains. The scattered vegetation gave way to bare rock, cracked and fissured and strewn with boulders that had crashed down from above. Here and there it had eroded into deep hollows like dimples; there were crevices and overhangs and crevasses . . . but no caves.

At last Richard puffed to a halt and turned to look back the way we'd come. 'I'd have expected to find the caves before this, Adam,' he muttered. 'I know you can't take the whole dragon thing too literally, but – well, he'd be a pretty strange dragon if his eyes were tangled up around his ears.'

He was right: there was no point in going any higher. Watching the others pick their slow way towards us through the rocks, I wondered if we could have missed the opening. It would be narrow; almost certainly well hidden, if it was the bolt hole of the exiled king.

Gen was behind the others, trailing wearily across a circular patch of smooth, bare rock. That was exactly where you'd expect the dragon's eyes to be . . . but it was the one place where the rock seemed smoothest. That, and another smooth, round indent way over at the foot of the other mountain. From my vantage point they looked like two giant dimples side by side . . .

'Rich!' I yelped. 'Look over there! It's not caves, but . . . d'you think those two hollows could be . . . empty sockets? And if they are –'

'Way to go, Adam! How does the poem go? *In empty sockets seek the prize that's hidden in the dragon's eyes!* That means the entrance to the caves – the eyes – must be down there somewhere!'

But it wasn't. We combed every bit of the area around the two hollows, and found nothing that could have hidden anything bigger than a mouse.

'I say we call it a day,' said Rich at last, when it was too dark to carry on. 'I'm bushed, and hungry enough to eat an elephant.'

'There's one other possibility,' said Gen reluctantly.

'What if the eyes are hidden by some kind of magic? What if there's something we need to do to reveal them?'

'And what if the pools of darkness are important after all?' said Jamie. 'Say they're clues that have to be solved in sequence, and we can't skip stages out? Then we're in totally the wrong place. There are no pools of anything anywhere – this entire area's as dry as a bone.'

There was a miserable silence. I looked round at the tired, grimy faces that had been so lit up with energy and excitement that morning. Now they were close to tears with exhaustion and disappointment.

'We've done all we can for now,' I said gently. 'Rich is right – let's have something to eat and get some rest. There was an overhang a bit higher up the slope; if it rains, it might give us some shelter.'

We dragged ourselves up to the shallow ledge and settled down under it with our backs to the rock. The long snout of the dragon stretched away from us, lit by the silver glow of the crescent moon rising over the plain.

But over the hidden valley a storm was building. Already it had bitten a black chunk out of the sky; as we watched, the bank of cumulus cloud was advancing, bulbous, bulging, gobbling the stars. Its edges rippled and pulsed with flickering blue light. I could smell the wall of pressure it was pushing before it: dense, slow-moving air reeking of raw electricity and hot rock.

There was a distant rumbling, a constant low vibration like a giant piece of furniture being slowly pushed towards us through the sky.

'Well,' I said reluctantly, hoping to distract the others from the grim reality of a wet night with no wood and no fire, 'I guess it's my turn to have a crack at that diary.'

I pulled it out and frowned down at the first page. The writing was there, faint and silvery and – for me – almost impossible to read. My guts twisted. Aside from writing, reading aloud was my worst. But if the others could do it, so could I.

My fingers fumbled with the flimsy pages, turning them clumsily till I reached the place where the writing changed; then past it, to where Kenta had left off. Zagros' writing was different from Zaronel's curving script: strong, upright strokes as easy as printing to read. *These are your friends*, I told myself. *It won't matter if you make the odd mistake.*

But the hollow feeling inside me had nothing to do with making mistakes. Some deep instinct told me that what I was about to read lay at the very heart of the mystery of Karazan . . . and that uncovering it would change everything forever.

POOLS OF DARKNESS

I position my finger under the first line to keep my place, take a deep breath, and begin. I read slowly, haltingly. The magic doesn't happen for me this time. There are no pictures: only words, bleak and full of pain, falling hard as stones on the bare mountainside.

King Zane is dead – we know by whose hand. Evor, roosting in his high tower like a raven, mixing his potions and poisons; Zeel, pretending friendship and brotherhood, slipping a deadly powder into a goblet of wine after the hard day's hunt.

I write by the moonlight that falls through the casement of the royal chamber. Meirion has told me it is my duty to set down the events of this night, that in the future all should not be lost to memory – but to what purpose? All is in ruin. The heir of Karazan and Antarion is yet unborn, but Zeel's soldiers stand guard outside the locked door of the chamber, awaiting his first cry.

I hear the sword being sharpened.

The queen has uttered no word since the passing of King

269

Zane. Her time is near, but her labour is silent. I pray it will be brief – as brief as will be the life of the infant prince. He is to be named Zephyr after the wind that bears him here; after the wind that will blow him hence, to the distant shores of the next world.

Meirion offers me words I know are meant as comfort. 'His passing will be but a passage into a different world, friend Zagros,' he tells me. 'A place where none will do him harm; a safe harbour, where his spirit will be free. Who knows? Perhaps one day he will return; for the door between the worlds is but a curtain that blows in the wind, as insubstantial as the mist.'

He whispers and murmurs to Zaronel as he ministers to her, though to what end I do not know. The fate of Prince Zephyr is sealed; he is lost before he draws breath. And what lies ahead for my lady I know to be, for her, a fate far worse than death.

Still I write on at the command of the mage. The night advances. The steel-shod boots of Zeel's men cross and re-cross before the door.

Once only has the queen spoken. Meirion called me to her. Her face was as pale as her pillow, seared with sorrow and pain; yet her eyes burned with a desperate hope. 'Do not despair, Zagros,' she whispered. 'All will not be lost. But the future rests with you, and you alone –' Her face twisted as another pain came upon her, and Meirion gestured me away.

Midnight approaches: the darkest hour.

At last I hear it: not a cry, but the whimper of a new-born. Meirion draws me to the bedside. I look down upon them: queen, widow, mother . . . and boy-child, suckling at her breast. I kneel before him: my prince; my king. There are tears upon my face.

At last the babe's eyelids droop and close; his lips release the nipple, and he sleeps. Zaronel presses a single kiss onto his brow. Meirion takes him, wraps him warmly for his first and final journey. Delivers him into my arms. I hold him close.

Mine, then, is to be the duty of delivering the sleeping infant up to the guards. Once well met and forever farewell, little prince. I look at Meirion, awaiting his signal.

He presses something into my hand.

I look down. King Zane's silver larigot gleams in my palm; beside it, the Sign of Sovereignty. The mage whispers of a secret passageway through the wall of the palace . . . of a hidden store of potion that will render us invisible as we make our way to the forbidden depths of Shadowwood.

He speaks of the sunrise on this day, the day of Sunbalance when night and day are equal, that will reveal a hidden portal in the Cliffs of Stone . . .

The moon is gone. A crack of thunder splits the sky; steel rods of rain batter the mountainside.

I stare blindly out. My eyes, like my thoughts, are bent inward.

At last the whole picture is revealed, an intricate tapestry that tells a tale with its beginning half a century ago; its ending . . . who knows where? And

271

somewhere in that complex pattern is this moment; these five children on a mountainside.

Five in one . . . and one in five.

There is only one thing that still doesn't make sense: how could more than fifty years telescope into only thirteen? And then Q's long ago words at Quested Court drift into my mind: *It's not surprising that the timeframe is different in Karazan. Common sense suggests that the passage of time in different dimensions is different too . . . that fifteen minutes here would correspond to an hour in Karazan . . .*

And finally I understand.

The storm passes.

I follow the others down to level ground again, where the deluge has filled the empty sockets of rock with rain. They are pools of darkness: the eyes of the dragon, staring up at the new-washed night sky. The others are babbling with excitement, laughing, calling out to me to hurry down, to run. Jamie is chanting the poem triumphantly, capering at the rim of the pool.

'*In pools of darkness seek to find
Zephyr, the lost Prince of the Wind;
In empty sockets seek the prize
That's hidden in the dragon's eyes.*'

I'm in no hurry. I know what we will find.

Gen's voice floats over to me as I move slowly closer, as if in a dream. 'Look – it's weird! The water really *is* dark – black, like ink. And though the moon's out, there are no reflections – none at all.'

They stand in a semi-circle round the pool, peering earnestly down at the blank water. 'Come and help us look, Adam. Maybe you'll see something we're missing . . .'

I take the last slow step to the edge of the pool. Kneel, and stare into the still water.

My own face stares back at me. Pale eyes, dark skin, a tangle of filthy hair. I am the same as ever . . . and at the same time, I am a stranger.

There is a faint radiance around my head, as if I am wearing a crown of stars.

Enter the parallel world of

KARAZAN

Half Boy
Half God
All Hero

'It's *Buffy* meets *Artemis Fowl*.
Thumbs up' – *Sunday Times*

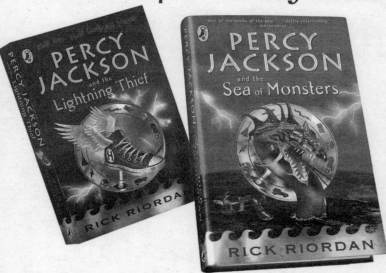

'A fast-paced, entertaining read'
– *Guardian*

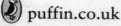